I0451217

GUNGE

Sunny Lewis

Copyright © 2025 by Sunny Lewis

All rights reserved.

No portion of this book may be reproduced in any form without written permission from the publisher or author, except as permitted by U.S. copyright law.

CONTENTS

FOR JAMIE, WHO LEFT US FAR TOO
SOON

CHAPTER ONE

GAS

It really wasn't hard for Bill and Bob Pletz to break into the office. They'd had plenty of experience picking locks and there was no alarm and no one around. They found one nitrous oxide tank in each of the three back rooms - their dentist did not like his patients to suffer. They wrestled one into the pickup, propped another against a wheel and had the third on the lip of the tailgate when Bob lost his grip and with a loud clatter it fell to the pavement, rolled down the incline and smashed into the gate. Instantly a Doberman appeared, its recessed gums revealing a large set of drooling teeth. A low murmur oozed from its throat.

"Holy shit, where the fuck did that come from?" Bill shrieked. "Just back away from him slowly, don't run!" he called out to Bob. "Nice doggy, nice little doggy, good little doggy, everything is fine, you're so cute, aren't you?" Bill inched open the driver-side door and was half inside when Bob backed into the tank that had been leaning against the wheel and it began its rapid descent to join its brother. The Doberman took off down the slope in pursuit, skidded splay-legged into the fence, bounced off and landed on top of the two tanks. Seizing one of the nozzles between its jaws, with a savage growl it began thrashing its head from side to side. Bob stood paralyzed, leaning like a board against the truck. "Bob!" Bill hissed. "What the hell are you doing? Get in the fucking cab!"

Silence. Bill climbed slowly out and crept back to the tailgate. "Where's the dog?" he whispered. He looked into his brother's blank face and slapped it hard. "Wake up!" Bob opened his eyes and began to shake.

"W-where's the dog?"

"You should know, you were out here, I was in the truck."

"Well, I don't know."

"Jesus, c'mon, it's not here now, let's get out of here while we can."

"What about the other two tanks, we can't just leave 'em," Bob whined.

"Oh, suddenly you're Mister Courage. You wanna go down there and give that hellhound a chance to latch onto your leg, be my guest. I'll just go home and start sucking on the one sure tank we actually have."

Bill got in the cab and started the engine. Bob kicked the truck. "I told you we should-a brought a gun."

"No, no firearms, ever. No damn guns. Wait a minute," he said, pulling a Louisville Slugger down from the gun rack. "That motherfucker tries anything I'll hit a home run with his goddamn head." He flipped Bob a beat-up glove.

"Here. You can catch it when it comes off."

Bob took a few hesitant steps down the driveway.

"Bill, we gotta torch?"

"A torch? What, you gonna burn down Frankenstein? You see any castles around here?"

"Nah, a torch is a flashlight, that's what they call it in England. It's gettin' dark and I don't wanna slip and fall again."

"Jesus Christ, then why didn't you just ask me for a goddamn flashlight, idiot?"

"It's fun to call it a torch like we're in England."

Bill shook his head. "You know, sometimes I really can't believe you're my brother. I really can't. There is something seriously the fuck wrong with you. This ain't no time for fun. When we get those tanks home I'll show you some fun. Now let's go!"

"Yeah, but do we have a torch? I mean a flashlight?"

Bill gave him a long look. "We do not have a flashlight," he said softly, emphasizing each word. "Use your phone."

"Oh, yeah, I forgot about that. Thanks, Bill!"

They started creeping carefully down the incline. Bob grabbed Bill's arm. "Wait a minute. He might see the light and come charging at us. You got the bat?"

"Yeah, I got the bat. You got the glove?"

"Man, you ain't gonna knock his head completely off. Even if you hit him with all your might it would just hang there, it wouldn't go flyin' off his body."

"You never know, I was a real slugger in Little League."

They continued slowly downhill. "Oh, yeah," Bob grinned, "remember when you hit that walk-off home run and it smashed the coach's car window and he didn't know whether to be happy or mad because we won the game and -"

"Shh. Shine that light down by the fence, I think I see something."

"Yeah, it looks like part of a tank. But what's that on top of it?"

"Oh, shit, that's the dog!"

"Let's get outta here, fuck the tanks!"

Bill grabbed the phone and edged closer to the fence. "He's out cold, man! Help me roll him off the tanks and we're Golden, Colorado."

"No way, that thing could wake up and tear us apart. Why don't you give him a good whack and put him out for keeps?"

"We're not gonna hurt an innocent creature. It's not his fault he's a ferocious fucking beast. He's just doing his job. You can take the rear end and I'll take the head so you won't have to worry about those teeth."

"Yeah, well, I'm not too crazy about his butt either, you know those things don't wipe their asses."

"Just grab his hind legs and roll him to the left. One, two, three, roll!"

When it hit the ground the dog shuddered and groaned but remained still. The boys checked both tanks, picked up the unopened one, stashed it next to the one they already had and sat in the cab a while, smoking a joint and congratulating themselves. Suddenly they burst into harmony on an old song they'd written years ago - "No more

worry, no more woe, we've got lots of N Two Oh!"
But by the time they pulled out of the parking
lot they were no longer alone. Humans aren't the
only creatures that enjoy getting high.

Chapter Two

JAILBAIT

She couldn't have been more than 16 years old and when she zipped past him on her scooter, Jimmy Hanson barely had time to reflect on what he'd seen: four and a half feet tall at the most, golden-brown skin, long hair fanning out behind her tiny doll face, her incongruously huge, braless breasts swaying back and forth as she wound her way through the pedestrians. Jesus H. Christ, he thought, that's the third one this week. Preternaturally developed schoolgirls loose on the summer sidewalks, turning heads from 9 to 90 because it's just impossible they could look like that. He stooped to light a cigarette against the wind and shook his head. I'll bet she puts out, too, he thought. Gettin' hit on all day long by those hormone-crazed boys and probably girls too. Wonder how she manages in the shower after gym class. There's so much gay shit going on these days and there's no way to conceal that body. A body I will never see again, he sighed. I could stand on this corner all day long for a week with nothing to show for it because today she just happened to be on her way to see a friend who's moving to California tomorrow and this is the first and last time for her to be going down this street. That would be just my luck. He threw his barely smoked Pall Mall to the sidewalk, lit another one and took a long drag. Just as well, he mused, exhaling into the warm breeze. If I got lucky I'd be out of luck. They'd throw my middle- aged butt straight in the can.

But in his desperate horny loneliness he found himself the next day right back on the busy corner of 125th Street and Lenox Avenue, leaning, smoking and watching. It wasn't long until something caught his attention. A very big balding African- American man in a track suit, back propped against the subway railing, began flailing his arms and stomping his feet, berating the government to nobody in particular. Everyone ignored him, including the slender Hispanic boy who hopped up onto the railing right beside him and began pumping his behind up and down on the spikes. After about a minute of this he jumped down and began walking gingerly and with considerable difficulty up Lenox Avenue. Once again Jimmy Hanson had to shake his head in wonder and as he was shaking and wondering a purple- afro-sporting girl walked into the boy's arms and they ambled off together up the street. Jimmy was so fixed on these two that he failed to notice the busty young scooter rider sail past in the opposite direction.

Chapter Three

JOHN

Robin's husband, arm splayed stiffly against the side of his leg, walked past the swimming pool of the Hilton where he and his wife were spending their vacation.

"Oh, my God, did John have a stroke?" their friend Anne asked.

"No," Robin replied, "he's holding his underpants up. They have to be very loose or they'll bother his stomach."

"Maybe he should just let them fall and give us a treat."

"Believe me it wouldn't be a treat."

***

John Camry slouched in the straight-backed chair and gazed at the nurse.

"Roll up your sleeve and let me put the needle in." She poked about and he grimaced. "I can't find a vein, they're all collapsed."

"That's what happens with twenty years of shooting smack," John joked. "Jesus, that hurts, try the other arm!"

"I'm so sorry" she whispered, softly stroking his hand.

"Careful, I could sue you for sexual harassment."

"Now who would believe a young girl like me would be interested in a wrinkled old man like you?"

"There's more to a man than youth and looks."

"Such as..."

"Such as steely resolve. Steely Dan resolve."

"Like Becker and Fagen?"

"No, like Burroughs' dildo."

When he got home he ripped the Band -Aid from his arm, sat down in his reclining chair, stretched out his long legs to the fullest and filled his pipe. "Women - who needs 'em?" he grumbled, "I've got my good old elf boys at my beck and call." He spun his Zippo and inhaled. Colors, swirling shapes, a crackling sound and he burst into his new favorite place.

***

(Taken from John Camry's sworn testimony to the New York City Police Department)

"Where've you been?" a group of little men called out to me in unison. "We've been waiting for you!" One of the taller of the elfin creatures, the leader, who I had learned on earlier trips was called Gunge, surged forward.

"Things look different," I said. "Everything seems a little simpler." Although the walls, if you can call them walls, were pulsing slightly, there was an absence of the usual hectic surfaces, spheres, undulating staircases, glowing balls, bursting bladders, shrieking crustaceans and other assorted psychedelic gymnastics that always stunned me into awe upon arriving among the little playful inhabitants of whatever this place was. I wasn't even sure it was a place. As I tried to explain countless times to my wife, it was too far outside normal human experience. Was it an actual world, another dimension, a parallel universe?

"Yes, it looks different," I repeated. "Everything's calmer."

"That's because we have something serious to show you," the elf replied. "But first, maybe this will make you feel more at home."

He jetted backward in an arc, slamming the top of his head into the twisting wall, which burst into thousands of spinning multi-colored diamonds that seemed to fill every inch of my field of vision and which, whirring at ever-increasing frequencies began to chant in numberless tongues, all of which I could somehow understand perfectly, "How's this? How's this? How's this? Do you like it? Do you like it? What is it? What is it? What is it? It it it it it it it it!" And then each voice assumed a different melody until my ears filled with a complete spectrum of harmony, the top notes emitting the aroma of roses, daffodils, night blooming jasmine, followed in swift succession by animal musk, swamp stench, vegetable rot, excrement, blood, bile, then roses again and everything morphed into brilliant rubies whose beating facets were somehow warm and loving.

Gunge smiled. "There, now. Feel better?" I tried to open my eyes to end the vision but they were locked shut. This had happened to me once before when things had grown intense. I focused on the feelings of warmth and love coming from the rubies and gradually regained my composure.

"Oh yeah, everything's just hunky-dory now, your excellency."

Gunge smiled again, his teeth burgeoning into gigantic tusks that shrank back to normal in an instant. "I'm so glad. Because now we really must get down to the serious business that brought you here in the first place."

"I didn't come to see you on any serious business, just for the usual nutcase festivities."

"And why did you visit us again after such a long absence?"

"I don't know, it was just a feeling that came over me."

"Exactly." The elf smiled again, but this time his teeth stayed at their normal size.

"Now watch this."

I saw myself walking past a swimming pool where my wife and her friend were sunbathing. They were talking about my underpants. "Hey," I said, that's from when I was on vacation in Miami a couple days ago!"

"Yes, it is," Gunge replied. "And were you doing any smoking at that time?"

"No, I'd left everything at home," I said and then it hit me. This had nothing to do with getting high, it was just one of the countless experiences stored in what I thought was my private, unassailable memory banks. The elf leader read my puzzled expression.

"Now do you get the picture? We have other abilities than fabricating languages and diamonds."

I noticed my hands had begun to shake. "Who are you guys anyway?" I blurted. "What are you really?"

"Don't worry about who or what we are," Gunge replied. "It's what we're not that matters."

(This concludes John Camry's written testimony)

Chapter Four

DR. MENDELSSOHN

Having given a couple quick kicks to the empty canister outside his office, Dr. Eugene Onegin Mendelssohn paused to stroke his beard. "E flat," he mused aloud, unleashing one more steel-toed blow and humming along to the echo. "Completely empty. Very strange." Inside he noticed the absence of the rest of his nitrous oxide supply. He made two phone calls, one to his receptionist, who was due to arrive shortly, to cancel all the day's appointments and the other to a locksmith to change the front door lock and install a security system. He did not call the police. He knew who the thieves were and would take care of them personally. He did wonder what had become of his dog, Bowser, but deciding not to dwell on the mystery climbed back behind the wheel of his 1983 Mercedes Benz and drove back home. There he poured himself a glass of Patron Tequila, took a beer from the refrigerator and opened the valve of one of the half dozen tanks he kept in the library. Two hours and a cigar later he was ready to confront the Pletz brothers.

Their doorbell's lightly swinging version of "Take it Easy" had barely got to the second measure before the doctor's face lit up with a smile as he recognized the wild barking of his dog, but the smile quickly turned into a scowl. "These boys have really gone too far this time," he groaned.

Bob opened the door and sheepishly backed his way back into the room, stumbling on Bowser, who shot past him and leapt onto his owner, covering the dentist's face with licks. "Bill, it's Dr. Mendelssohn!" Bob called to his brother.

"Oh, shit, man, I'm so sorry," Bill began before Mendelssohn had even entered the house. "I don't know why the fuck we did that, you've always treated us right. We didn't know you got a dog, man, we didn't kidnap him or nothing, when we got home we found him in the back of the truck. He must have jumped in there before we left. He was snuggled up to the tanks all nice and peaceful like." He lurched off the couch. "You want a beer? We got everything - Pabst, Bud, Bud Light, Rolling Rock, we got some whiskey. You want a shot?"

The doctor made his way slowly to the couch and sat down on the arm, looking at the floor. For a long time no one spoke. Bob stood in the middle of the room chewing his lip. Bill returned to the couch, sat on the other arm and joined Mendelssohn in staring at the floor. Mendelssohn raised his head. "First of all I want you to know I'm not mad at you. But I am disappointed. Very disappointed. Since the accident I think I've done my best to always look out for you and to be there when you needed me. That's what your dad would have wanted and I think that based on the friendship we had, that's what he would have expected of me. And I've been happy to do it. He was my best friend ever since childhood and except for the sear sucker suits, I had a lot of respect for the man. I mean, sear sucker suits when the weather's hot, OK, but all winter long too?" (The brothers snickered.) "You boys have not been saints by any stretch of the imagination but I thought you at least had a good concept of right and wrong. Now I'm beginning to wonder if you do. That's why I'm disappointed. And I'm disappointed because you haven't just let me down you've let your parents down as well and they were good people who deserve better than that." Mendelssohn stood, walked to the bedroom and glanced inside. "Here," he said to

26

Bob, tossing him his keys. "Put those tanks in the trunk of my car. C'mon, Bowser."

CHAPTER FIVE

THE GAME

The next night was Mendelssohn's weekly poker game. It attracted local players and was often held in the dentist's sprawling house, but only when he didn't have a live-in girlfriend, as he knew from experience she would threaten to leave him when she saw how rowdy things could get. He enjoyed having company and didn't mind being the go-to host, which was a boon to the tradition's longevity, as no one else was willing to take the helm.

On this occasion he had managed to put the discouraging contretemps of the day before in the back of his mind and was, as usual, having a good time. He looked fondly around the table at the friends he had known for so many years, some of them rocks he could trust to have his back in any situation and others stalwarts but only of the fair weather variety. Among the former was his cousin Charles, also a dentist, and Jack French, whom he'd known for most of his life and who'd saved his ass on more than one occasion in their wild adolescent years. Tony Bunson, tavern owner and dabbler in various other areas of endeavor, was not someone Mendelssohn was particularly eager to spend time with at the poker table; though a new addition to the group, Bunson had already managed to get into some virulent arguments and was generally considered to be on probation.

At this night's gathering Bunson was staring stone-faced toward the end of the table, where John Camry and Jack French were engaged in an intense conversation, John poking Jack lightly on the chest to emphasize his words. "OK, here's one for you. If you had the ability to end all life on Earth with the push of a button and everyone would die instantly, with no suffering and no survivors feeling the pain of losing their loved ones, and in addition you would never be blamed for it, would you do it?"

Jack slapped his friend's finger away from his chest. "What, are you nuts? Why the hell would I wanna do something like that? You're fucking crazy!"

"No, no, you don't get it! What about all the suffering? It would be over forever! No more pain, no more hunger, no more broken hearts! You'd be the salvation of all mankind!"

"No more pain, no more hunger, no more broken hearts, yeah. But also no more children, no more sex, no more friendship, no more oceans and mountains and sunsets. Jesus, John, I know you've been depressed but you gotta see there's a lot of good things about life too."

"OK, OK, what about this" John continued, raising his finger in Jack's direction but hastily dropping it as Jack countered with his own. "You're literally at death's door, it's like Let's Make a Deal and you have two doors to choose from. One door will take you to a guaranteed afterlife but you have no way of knowing whether it'll be heaven or hell, or whether you'll be judged on everything you've done in your life and forgiven regardless of how bad you've been. The other door is certain oblivion - there will be no afterlife at all - no suffering, but also no possibility of meeting up with your dead friends and relatives, no harps and angels, no blissful paradise. Just nothing. No you, no consciousness. Nothing."

By now the card game had completely ground to a halt as all the players were raptly following the conversation. Tony Bunson couldn't take any more and jumping to his feet he yanked the cigar out of his mouth. "Hey!" he yelled. "Are you fuckheads playing cards or playing philosopher? I got a lot of money riding on this hand and I'm sick of waiting on you jerks to stop your goddamn blabbering. Now are you in or are you out?"

John picked up a card and waved it like a fan in Tony's direction. "Relax, Tony, chill out. We're just having a little speculative discussion here. I'm in. I'll see your hundred and raise you another two. Whaddya got, motherfucker?"

The arc of cards, chips and money that Tony set in motion paralleled the path of his luck that night. Everything went high in the air and fell quickly to the floor. If he hadn't lifted and flung the table what some later claimed was four or five feet into the air, a feat powered by a rage that for some time had been boiling just below the surface, his 3 ace-2 king full house would have won him a couple thousand dollars, a record high for games played at Dr. Mendelssohn's. As it turned out, it would be a long time before Tony Bunson would be a member of this group and the next time the friends met up, without Tony, it would be for a different purpose.

Chapter Six

ANNA

Anna Jones could have hopped on her scooter and zipped to any number of dentists in Manhattan within minutes but she preferred to take the long L train ride out to Ridgewood to see Dr. Mendelssohn. If asked whether it was for the liberally dispensed gas or because of her crush on the doctor she would certainly say it was both, as her inability to lie vied seriously with her youthful appearance for the honor of most salient trait. She was, however, nowhere near as young as her Lenox Avenue admirer, Jimmy Hanson, believed. Yes, he was right that she was a student, but in grad school, not high school. At 28 she was, in fact, older than most of her classmates.

For this particular appointment she decided to try an experiment. After a long walk up DeKalb Avenue, as she neared the office she lit up a joint. By the time she arrived she had three tokes in her system, the last of which she exhaled into Bowser's slobbering face as he danced up to greet her. He seemed to like it.

The office was empty. Anna followed the hygienist into the back room and shook hands with Mendelssohn, who smiled. "So you're finally coming around to let me take care of that root canal you've been putting off for so long?"

She put on her headphones and pressed play on her phone. "Just keep that gas coming is all I ask."

When she opened her eyes the doctor handed her a paper cup. "Rinse," he said, daubing with a towel around her mouth. She spit some blood into the bowl. "Jesus, that was fantastic!"

"Yeah, I thought I did a pretty good job on a pretty tough tooth. But you were practically out cold, so how would you know?"

"Not the tooth, Charlie Parker," she replied. "He hit this one note, one low note and his whole life went through me. I knew him, I mean I really knew him. I swear I felt his soul."

Mendelssohn gave her a puzzled look. "I know sweet air helps you relax and forget about the drill, but I've never heard of a reaction like that."

Anna laughed. "I'll tell you a little secret, Doc. I read that combining pot and nitrous oxide could take you to a new level you can't get to doing them separately. Guess what. It's true!"

Mendelssohn puffed out his cheeks. "Charlie Parker, eh? Dizzy gave him a good run for his money but Bird was in another category. He was like the Beatles of the jazz world - head and shoulders above everyone else."

Anna cocked her head. "So you're familiar?"

"Damn straight I'm familiar. Bebop's by favorite kind of music."

"Ya know, Charlie wouldn't like you saying that. He probably agreed with Louis Armstrong that you can't pigeonhole music; there's only two categories of music, good and bad."

"There's no doubt which category Charlie belongs in," Mendelssohn replied. Their eyes locked in silence for a good ten seconds. Mendelssohn shuffled his feet and cleared his throat. "You know what I think might be fun? We should go out to dinner some time."

Anna put her hand on her heart and leaned back dramatically in her chair.

"But Dr. Mendelssohn, isn't it strictly forbidden for a doctor to have a personal relationship with a patient?"

Mendelssohn grinned. "I'm not a doctor. I'm a dentist."

Chapter Seven

THE DATE

Anna left her scooter in her Washington Heights apartment and took a cab down to 127th and Lenox. I may look like a kid, she thought, but maybe it's time to stop acting like one. Her date was already sitting at a table when she walked into the Lenox Saphire. "I really feel like a jerk not picking you up like a proper gentleman," he said.

"What, come all the way in from Queens, go farther uptown and then have to come back down again? That's ridiculous. I'm a big girl, women are looking out for themselves now and we don't need men to take care of us anymore."

Mendelssohn rose slowly to his feet and began putting on his coat. "I'm sorry, I, uh, I guess I made a mistake." He straightened his tie and headed for the door.

"What are you doing!"Anna barked. "Can't you tell when someone's pulling your leg? Get back here!" Before he had time to react she was out of her chair and holding his hand. "I'm an idiot," she whispered. "Please forgive me. Please come back to the table. "He allowed himself to be led by the hand back to his chair.

Putting his elbows on the table he shook his head.

"I really don't know what to make of you."

Anna fiddled with the salt shaker. "I don't know what to make of me either. I'm always putting my foot in my mouth and ruining things. It's been this way ever since I can remember. Instead of thinking I just blurt out whatever's in my head and then spend a year trying to explain myself but since even I don't know why I do this shit it's impossible to make anyone else understand."

Mendelssohn took the salt shaker from her hand and rapped it on the table in time with his words. "I'm. Not. Just. Any. One. Else." He tilted the container on its side and rocked it back and forth. "I'm your dentist. And as such I have so many tricks up my sleeve. I'll bet you've never seen this done before." Pouring a few grains of salt on the table he edged the shaker delicately between them. "Et voila," he proclaimed, letting go. The shaker balanced for a split second then tumbled on its side and the cap fell off, spilling salt out across the table.

"Hoo whee!" shouted Anna, clapping her hands. "Now you've gone and done it!" Oblivious to the stares from the other tables she partially cleared a space and tilted the salt container onto the remaining grains. Slowly she removed her hands. The shaker stayed balanced on its edge and a group of teenagers sitting a few feet away burst into applause. "That's showin' 'em sister!" one called out. Anna rose and bowed, glanced at Mendelssohn and quickly sat back down. "Didn't mean to show you up, Doc, we've been doing that one in my family for years. Anyway, do you wanna just run or should we clean up this mess and have something to eat?"

Rising dramatically from his chair and proclaiming, "Ladies and gentlemen, I shall now with this magic cloth make disappear all faux pas which have been committed here tonight," Mendelssohn threw a look at Anna, pulled his napkin from his sleeve and tossed it onto the scattered salt. "Waiter!" he yelled, "could we please have another table? I'm afraid my friend here has made a bit of a disaster of this one."

Chapter Eight

JOHN BY NIGHT

N ow I lay me down to snooze I pray tonight my life I lose there's a lovely world that's waiting for me a lovely world I can't wait to see where my Dad and my aunts uncles grandmas and gramps are waiting they're waiting for me. Sometimes avocados skip the ripe stage they go right from unripe to rotten I am so looking forward to getting out of this body you just blast off to that better world. Lying there staring at the ceiling waiting for the sleepy feeling sleep the little death not big enough you always wake up. A lot of walking today my foot didn't hurt what a lucky break wrong I'm not happy because my foot didn't hurt doesn't help a bit.

This is from hating everything everything sucks so why not hate it. How staggeringly wonderful it would be to die in my sleep tonight oh god how I wish I was dead but I never die. Ah I see you are preparing your death bed yes each night I beg the lord to take me into his loving arms he never does. Now I lay me down to snooze I pray tonight my life I lose.

Chapter Nine

JOHN BY DAY

Twisting and turning viciously, kicking his legs frantically under the sheets, John propped himself up on one arm and with the other hurled his pillow across the room. "Son of a motherfucking bitch!" he yelled. "I am not going to get up. No fucking way. Why why why?" He lay back down and buried himself under the blanket but he knew it was hopeless. His whole body was quivering and even if he'd had the pillow there was no possibility of going back to sleep. It's always this way, he sighed - facing the day is inevitable. He limped into the bathroom, took a seat and turned on the radio. The static that resulted made it impossible to understand a word. He felt an immediate urge to smoke.

"What took you so long?" the elves called out. The leader blossomed from a crystal in the wall and loomed in John's face. "We don't like being kept waiting. You didn't have to do all that ugly wiping and showering and eating your stupid blueberries before coming to see us. Don't you like us? Haven't we always been good to you?"

John shrugged. "I guess so. I mean you're never boring but you're also a little frightening."

"Oh, are we?" Gunge leered, turning into a drooling wolf.

"Yeah, that's what I'm talking about," John replied in a steady voice.

The wolf morphed back. "You don't seem very frightened to me."

"That's 'cause I'm starting to get a little tired of your shenanigans. It's not as much fun coming here anymore."

Gunge almost looked sad. "You're a very unhappy man, aren't you?"

"Everyone is unhappy."

"That may be true but you seem to be further along than most. You wish you'd never been born."

"That's ridiculous,I've never expressed any feelings to you, positive or negative, other than how awed I am by your insanely surreal world. You know nothing about me."

"We don't? Remember that little swimming pool scene we showed you? How did you wind up coming to us again today? Just felt like having a little smoke?"

"I don't know, I was just listening to the radio and suddenly I felt the urge. Hey, that's what happened the last time. Out of the blue I felt like it was so important to smoke."

"Yes, you see we are constantly improving our abilities."

"You can't affect things in my world. You're just a trapped figment of my imagination."

"Are we? You have no idea where we are and what we can and cannot do." The leader sprouted a villain's mustache with self-twirling ends. "Look ma, no hands."

"Parlor tricks," John snorted.

"OK, how about this one?" A giant frog, a darting tongue, one less elf.

John recoiled. "Tell me you didn't just eat your friend?"

"I wouldn't exactly call it eating and I wouldn't exactly call him my friend."

"Jesus, you are really disgusting."

Gunge smiled. "This disgusting guy could be your best buddy."

"After what you just did I don't think I want to be your buddy."

"Oh, yes you do. You want very much to be my buddy. I can make you very happy."

"Yeah, you used to make me happy but now I'm beginning to regret that I ever started smoking that shit."

Gunge's face assumed a concerned and caring appearance. "I'm talking about happy in your world, the world you hate with, as you like to say, every fiber of your being. How would you like to have all the things you crave? Money, power, respect, women? Would you still want to die if you had those?"

Standing up John folded his arms and rocked back and forth on his heels. "You can't give me those things, you can't do business in my world, you're trapped here in whatever the hell this place is, maybe hell itself I'm beginning to think."

"You keep telling me I'm trapped," Gunge smirked, "and I keep showing you I'm not. Why not play along with me? What've you got to lose?"

"Just tell me what the fuck you want from me."

"I want to meet your friends."

CHAPTER TEN

A PFFFFT, A POEM, A POSSIBILITY AND A PHONE CALL

"Do you like when I wrap my long black hair around your cock like this and then I squeeze?"

"Mwaah."

"Do you like when I unwrap it ever so slowly like this?"

"Mwaaah."

"Do you like when I wrap it back again and squeeze a little harder like this?"

"Mwaaah wuhh oh oohoooh oooh oooh ahhhh...Sorry..."

"Oh my God, you've come all over my hair!"

"Jesus, babe, I'm so sorry, I got to the edge and I thought I could ride it but I just couldn't hold it back."

Anna smirked. "The good doctor, indeed. Now I have to wash my hair."

Mendelssohn sighed.

"Hey," Anna said, "it's alright, I had to wash it anyway," and swinging her feet over the bed she padded off to the bathroom. "I want you to think about what a bad boy you've been," she called over her shoulder. "A bad bad boy." The doctor lit a joint and did not think about what a bad boy he had been but about what a good boy he could be.

When Anna returned from the bathroom with nothing on but a towel around her head and sat down on the bed he pinched her nipples and pleaded, "Let me make it up to you."

She slapped his hand away. "You know you really have been a bad boy and I don't mean because of your ejaculatio praecox. I still haven't forgiven you for making fun of me in the restaurant. That's not what a gentleman does on a first date. Not on any date, for that matter." She eyed his crotch. "But I'm going to give you a break because I'm such a good sport, people have always told me I'm a good sport." She smiled. "And I'm feeling particularly horny right now seeing as how you seem to be sincere in your intentions.

Mendelssohn smiled in turn. "People have always told me I'm sincere," he said and pulled her down to his side.

***

Leaning back on the bedstead the "good doctor" took a toke on the leftover roach, passed it to Anna and croaked, "Now, aren't you glad you gave me a second chance?"

She took a deep hit and held it for so long he began to worry. "Hey, everything's been absorbed by now, you have to breath, you know."

Coughing maniacally she barked a double lungful of smoke and burst out laughing.

"You don't know wh- what you're talking abu-bout," she sputtered between coughs. "Look at all that smoke!"

"But I'm telling you all the THC had already been absorbed," he replied.

"How do you know?"

"I just know."

"No, you don't, you're not an expert on chemistry, you're just a dentist."

"Just a dentist, eh? And what are you?"

"But I'm still a student, I haven't decided what to do yet. And I'm just kidding, there's nothing wrong with being a dentist. Unless you enjoy causing pain, and you're

the least painful dentist I know."

"Gee, thanks, I'll treasure that comment always." He reached under the bed.

"Hey, you wanna read a poem?"

"Uh, sure."

He passed her a Post-it. "Read it out loud so you get the full poetic effect."

"If you insist." She squinted. "God, your handwriting is atrocious. OK, I'll try to read it. Here goes. "Bullhorns blasting, a contingent of feather-wearing Freemasons cleared the road of cock-a-doodle-doos." She looked up at the ceiling. "What the heck is that supposed to mean? That's not a poem!"

"Sure it is,"Mendelssohn retorted.

"It's only one line!"

"Who says a poem has to have more than one line?"

"But what does it mean? It's complete nonsense!"

"It means whatever you want it to mean."

"Well, I don't know what I want it to mean because it's complete nonsense, how can I make it mean something when it's nonsense?"

"Listen, lots of classic poems were originally thought to be complete nonsense, but now it's common knowledge that - is that my phone or yours? It's mine, I better get this, it could be one of my patients in dire need of my services."

"Yeah, in dire need of some opioids for some pain he's not in so he can get high."

"Hey, that's not fair, I'm very strict when it comes to my patients' drug use.

Hello. Yeah, hi, John, what's up? Sure, sounds like fun. Let me know when. Alright, you take it easy too. See you soon."

"Who's John?"

'Oh, he's a patient of mine. Says he's come across a new drug he wants me to check out."

Chapter Eleven

NEW INITIATE

"Jesus, what the hell just happened?" Mendelssohn's pipe slipped from his hand and bounced from the couch to the floor. "Who are those people? Are they people? Where was I? Was that some kind of palace?"

John grinned. "I knew you'd like it, man!"

"Now it's starting to fade," the doctor sighed, "like a dream. But I know it wasn't a dream, it was absolutely real and I was really there. But it's impossible, there were all these weird shapes and jewels and some of them were people and they were talking and I understood them but it wasn't like normal talking and I don't even know if it was in English but I definitely could understand them and it's just so fucking confusing!"

"Hey, take it easy there, Mendy old boy, finish your beer!"

Mendelssohn took a sip and followed it with noisy gulps, draining the glass.

"Christ, I needed that. Mind if I have another?"

"Help yourself," John laughed. "There's plenty in the fridge. Get drunk if you want to."

But the doctor did not get drunk. He wanted to remain clear-headed to analyze what had just happened. He went home and lay in the dark on his bed. He laughed and said out loud, "I don't even know what the hell that drug is called!" He texted John. DMT. He googled it and began to read.There was plenty of material online but he knew what he really had to get was "DMT: The Spirit Molecule" by Rick Strassman and any and everything by Terence McKenna. And he had to get back into that other world as soon as possible.

Chapter Twelve

SOME OF THE OLD GANG GET TOGETHER AGAIN

Amped up from hours of reading, Mendelssohn made phone calls and convinced a few of his poker pals to meet for a "surprise-filled evening of fun and frolic."

Everyone agreed, "as long as Tony Bunson isn't invited," and reassured there was "no chance in hell of that ever happening again," they all showed up at 9 o'clock on Friday night at John Camry's. The Pletz brothers came too, both dressed in denim pants, shirts and jackets despite the 90 degree heat. Bill added a denim visor, hitched up his chair and plopped his elbows on the dining room table.

"Who's got the cards? And how come we're playing at John's? I know about your poker games and they're almost always played at your place, Doc."

"No cards tonight, boys, we've got bigger fish to fry."

"Nuts, I knew it was too good to be true that we were finally gonna get a chance to win a little moolah off you rich guys."

"You won't be winning any money and there won't be any hearts, spades or clubs but I guarantee you're gonna see more diamonds than you've ever imagined in your wildest dreams,"Mendelssohn replied. "As a matter of fact, you may very well think you are dreaming but I assure you what you *are* about to experience goes way beyond the usual dreamworld," he added.

Bob took off his jacket. "OK, I'm game for anything, but can we please get on with it? And can you turn up the AC?"

***

Ten minutes later the room was solidly divided between two camps: John Camry and Eugene Mendelssohn, who were sitting on the couch with shit-eating grins and the DMT neophytes: the Pletz brothers, Charles Grove and Jack French, who were wandering the living room and shaking their heads.

Bill Pletz was the first to speak. "OK, what the fuck was that?"

John raised his hands and rotated his arms in big circles. "Bwah! You tell me! Right, Mendy? We have no idea what's going on in that world. Whadda you think, Chuck old sport? Chuck?"

Charles, who had lain down on his back on the floor, was breathing loudly through his mouth.

Mendelssohn hurried over and lifted his cousin's head. "You all right, buddy? Want some water?"

"Beer," he croaked. Still on his back he drained the offered bottle and slowly sat up.

"I wasn't ready for that. You could have told us what to expect and given us some kind of a warning."

"Hey, man, I'm really sorry. I wanted it to be a surprise but I know you're not in the best of health and I'll admit that was really stupid of me."

"It's alright, just get me another beer. I gotta wash that shit outta my head."

Chapter Thirteen

JOHN VENTS

John Camry, on the other hand, was eager to get right back into it, and as soon as everyone had left, fired up his pipe again. Gunge greeted him effusively,his eyes not just sparkling, but physically sending off sparks, which streamed out to form a rotating halo around John's head. "Johnny my boy, what a lovely surprise! Why, we've only just parted yet here you are back with us again so soon. Isn't that wonderful!"

"Alright, cut the bullshit, Gunge, I did what you asked, I brought you my friends, now when are you gonna keep your end of the bargain? The money, the women, the power. Remember?"

"But John, I'm not a magician, I can't just snap my fingers and grant wishes like a genie. Your friends have only just left!"

"What the hell are you talkin' about, motherfucker! You can do anything! Look at these stupid sparks flying around and driving me crazy! It didn't take you more than half a second to start that shit when you saw me!"

Gunge laughed. "You don't like the sparks? They're gone!" And they were.

"You see, that's what I'm talkin' about. You can make things happen instantaneously. So I want the shit you promised me. Now!"

"John, it's only in my world I can do that. Making things happen in your world is uncharted territory, it's going to take time."

"Christ, Gunge, I don't have time! I'm behind on my rent, I'm thousands of dollars in debt, I'm barely able to put food on my own table, food for one skinny little person. But you know what? I could almost handle that shit anyways if I had a woman, but my wife hasn't given me so much as a hand job in eons. Do you have any idea how long it's been since I was with a woman?" Gunge shook his head. "I don't either, motherfucker, that's how fucking long it's been! I walk the streets staring at them like a lunatic, longing for eye contact, which hardly ever happens, but when it does, do I do anything about it? Of course not, I'm so fucking shy and lacking in self confidence I feel ashamed I even bothered them by looking at them. And they're so beautiful and desirable! Not all of them, in fact, very few, there's so many ugly ones too, I can't believe anyone would want to have sex with them but maybe there are guys who are even more desperate than me. I let 'em have it under my breath when they go by because even the ugly ones ignore me.

"You're fat! I say, you're too old, you look like an idiot, *ni me mires*, that's Spanish and means don't even look at me 'cause that's what my friend Rooster used to say when an ugly one gave him the eye on the street down in South America. But like I said, even if they're ugly they don't look at me anyway, I just say that from frustration, but I don't really care about them, it's the hot ones that kill me 'cause I want them so bad and they're so unattainable. They come about one in every three hundred, that's how rare they are, like diamonds, even more beautiful than the diamonds you create, so tell me you can create them in my world, gorgeous diamond women who want only me. I only need one, Gunge, just one!"

"And I only need one too," Gunge replied. "Bring me Anna Jones."

Chapter Fourteen

ANNA COMES ABOARD

Anna had just posed the question, "Would you like to lick my pussy?" to Dr. Mendelssohn when his phone rang. "Sorry, honey, I really have to take this."

"Just don't answer it, for crying out loud!"

"Now, I've told you many times that I am a doctor and I have to take my phone calls because my patients are very important to me."

"And I'm not, I suppose. And I already told you and you said so yourself, you're not a doctor, you're a dentist!"

"Right, right, we've already discussed that and it's meaningless. You know very well that I care about you very much but this could be an emergency and your vagina can wait a couple of minutes. Put your panties back on, it's very distracting."

He dodged Anna's airborne pillow. "Hey, John, always good to hear from you but this is a very inopportune time. I'm a little busy. What's up? Uh, yeah, that could work, I'll ask her. Alright, take it easy. Bye."

"You'll ask who what?"

"Take your panties off."

***

When Anna woke up the next morning her vagina was sore. But that wasn't what really bothered her. She couldn't quite remember what had happened the night before, only that she and Mendelssohn had gone over to his friend John's place and had done something weird. Slowly her mind began to clear but things were still a little foggy and she felt frustrated that she couldn't zero in on what had happened. Oh, no, not an orgy! she thought, but decided there was no way she and Gene would have got involved in something like that. It was drugs, yes, that sounded more like it,but why was her memory about it so hazy? She eased out of bed and meandered toward the bathroom. "When -he- comes- home- from- work- I'll -just have -to-ask -old- lover- boy- just -what -the- hell- we -got- into- last -night," she sang out loud in staccato as she stepped into the shower.

When Mendelssohn got home that evening she was still in her bathrobe, drinking tea in bed. "Hey honey, what's wrong, you feel alright? Didn't you go to your classes today?"

"No, I don't feel alright and I didn't go to classes."

"What is it, do you have a cold or something? I hope it's not the flu, there's a lot going around."

"I don't know what it is, I just don't feel well. What exactly did we do yesterday? I feel like I had a bad dream but I can't remember anything about it."

"Well, we had a really good time right about where you're situated right now, maybe a foot or two to the left, but then there was a lot of rolling around so I couldn't really pinpoint the exact location."

"Oh, come on, that's not what I'm talking about and you know it. I remember that perfectly well. I think we kind of overdid it to tell you the truth, I'm feeling a little uncomfortable down there."

"I have an excellent gel that would soon put all that discomfort out of your pretty little nether section, for a while at least. Then it might feel a little worse."

"You just stay away from me, I had plenty enough of your gel yesterday and it was the making of that gel that's at fault."

"Well, you know there are other ways of exceptionally painless manufacture, and then it could be applied as a soothing ointment."

"The only soothing I'm interested in is of my mind as to what else we did other than have sex."

"Babe, are you telling me you honestly can't remember that we went over to John's and smoked DMT?"

Anna clapped her hands. "Ah, now we're getting somewhere! That's right, you didn't tell me what it was but you said, 'Take a toke of this and you'll be absolutely amazed.'" She slid out of bed and began walking slowly around the room. "Well, I'm amazed alright, absolutely amazed that I can't remember anything after that. What the hell is DMT?"

"You mean you really have no recollection of visiting the fabulous world of the dwarves or of watching TV when we got home, having a couple beers and then going to bed super early because you said you were insanely exhausted?"

"Wait a minute, backup, whaddya mean the fabulous world of the dwarves? Did we go out to some weird club or something after we left John's, 'cause I kind of remember watching TV but I don't think it was Snow White."

"Ok, everybody has a little blackout with DMT, but this is ridiculous. I think you should have another go at it. If you're totally drawing a blank it's like you never had the experience at all, and it's just a waste. Whaddya say, wanna have another stab at it?"

"Alright, I guess so," Anna sighed. "And I meant what I said about no sex for a while."

"That's fine, we'll go over to John's and have another smoke. DMT is better than sex anyway."

"Oh, well screw you, mister!"

"No, I mean better than sex in general, not better than sex with you! Nothing could be better than sex with the smartest, classiest, hottest little gal in all of New York City."

"Yeah, right, nice recovery there, doctor. If only my pussy could recover that fast."

Chapter Fifteen

WOMAN OVERBOARD

Gunge was overjoyed to see Anna again. She'd been unreceptive on her first visit but he felt this session went extraordinarily well. Mendelssohn was also pleased, glad that his girlfriend, who, as they were driving home seemed to remember at least something of the experience this time, but he was puzzled by her lack of astonishment at encountering the sights and sounds that never failed to blow his mind whenever he smoked. "You saw the talking diamonds and weird little people and incredible colors and stuff,right?" he asked.

"Yeah, it was pretty cool."

"Pretty cool? Jesus, that shit is literally out of this world, it's beyond human comprehension, it's way beyond just cool! I guess you really managed to take the dwarves' advice not to be too awed by everything and just enjoy it, eh?"

"Yeah, I think they said something like that, I don't remember a whole lot, it's kind of hazy like it was the first time. There was one guy who seemed to be the head honcho, I know I spent some time with him but I'm not really sure what he said. Like I said, it's kind of hazy."

"OK, well at least you got something out of it this time. That's an improvement."

The next day Anna dropped out of school. I didn't much like NYU, I'm still young and I can go somewhere else some day if I feel like it, but for now I just wanna have fun, she told herself. To get out of the apartment and kill time she started riding her scooter any and everywhere, usually heading down through Harlem via Lenox Avenue to 125th Street, enjoying the stares and startled expressions she left in her wake, laughing at the occasional shouts of "Hey, watch where the fuck you're going! Get off the goddamn sidewalk!" when she cut it too close to an irate pedestrian. When she got to 125th she hopped off her scooter and went into the CVS there through the door on the Lenox side of the street. As was his custom, Jimmy Hanson was standing a few feet away from that door. His knees began shaking and he felt his scrotum tighten.

Holy shit! he thought. I can't fucking believe this. It's her. Again. I have to follow her and try to fill my head with her so I'll never forget what she looks like. Oh man oh man OK here goes, I have to do this or I'll never forgive myself. OK c'mon c'mon let's go let's do this don't be such a fucking coward you're just going to look at her you're not going to talk to her you've got nothing to lose but your own self esteem of which you have none anyways you fucking idiot so let's go.

He went in and scanned the front of the store. Nothin' here, he muttered to himself, no good-looking chicks at all, not even that one decent looking cashier they have, I swear this fucking place hires on the basis of whether the applicant is ugly enough. He walked slowly down the right hand aisle. She's in the rear, maybe at the pharmacy, he thought. That would be great, that would mean she gets her prescriptions here and she'll definitely be coming back. When he reached the shampoo display he crossed over to the left and peered down aisle 10. Yes! What a break, she's in line at the pharmacy! He moved closer and pretended to be looking at the vitamins while keeping an eye and ear on the girl and the cashier. "We have your Ativan," he heard the cashier say, "but the Prozac hasn't arrived yet, it should be here by tomorrow." "Oh boy oh boy, guess who else will be here tomorrow," he whispered to a row of half priced vitamin E. He stood there frozen, mind racing into the future as he fantasized on what it would be like to be with a super hot chick for the first time in his life. When he snapped out of it and turned toward the pharmacy Anna was buried in her phone and rapidly coming his way. She looked up and their eyes met. As she passed and gazed back over her shoulder, Jimmy felt himself go instantly hard.

Chapter Sixteen

JIMMY BY NIGHT

This is impossible. There's no way I'm gonna be able to sleep. I better take an Ativan. Jesus, I can't believe she takes that shit too. What a coincidence! Wonder what else we have in common. Nothing. Hell, she's a fucking high school student, for Christ sakes. Reading. Maybe she likes to read. Movies. Netflix. Smokin' weed. Now you're talkin'. But sex, that's the big one. She's gotta be into sex lookin' like that. And she's gotta be at least 17. Please, please God let her be at least 17. But man, I don't know, I think I'd risk jail time for that action if it came right down to it. And she's a little pigeon-toed and knock-kneed too. I love it when a beautiful woman is like that. It brings the angel down to earth just a little bit and somehow makes her even more attractive, I don't know why. Shit, I'd be willing to die for one night with a hot babe like that. Before they could lock me up I'd kill myself, it'd be worth it. Fuck, the way she looked at me! So intense! I still can't believe that. Did it really happen? OK, a little sleep dope. Maybe I'll have a dream about her...

Chapter Seventeen

Jimmy by Day

Jimmy did not have a dream about Anna, but it seemed she'd been in his head the whole night, as even with the Ativan he'd barely slept and he'd been unable to stop thinking about her. "I should have taken a whole one instead of just a half," he groaned, climbing slowly out of bed. "But now I can take the other half before I go to CVS 'cause I'm gonna need it bad. Maybe I should have a few beers too to calm me down and give me some courage. Nah, that might not be such a good idea, beer breath does not usually make a good first impression, except maybe with alcoholics. Shit, what time should I get there? The same time as yesterday, people are creatures of habit. Maybe a little early just in case.

At 2:30 he was in the store, pacing the aisles to work off his nerves, turning his head left and right like a lighthouse until his neck hurt enough that he finally resigned himself to camping out in his old spot by the vitamins. And there she was, already at the pharmacy and picking up her bag. He kicked himself in the foot.

Fuck, how the hell did she get past me? I'm not ready, I can't do this, I don't know what to say! But now he was trapped because Anna was standing directly in front of him and looking straight into his eyes.

"Did you get your Prozac?" he blurted out.

"Do I know you?"

"You ever go to Record Explosion on Fifth Avenue? I used to work there."

Anna shook her head and frowned. "How do you know I take Prozac?"

"I've been keeping a good eye on you. You've been looking a little depressed. I'm here to cheer you up."

"You some kinda stalker?"

"Nah, actually I just happened to be here yesterday and I overheard the cashier telling you to come back today for your Prozac. I really wanted to meet you, especially after that look you gave me."

"What look?"

"Don't you remember I was standing right here and you came by and stared at me while you were walking past?"

"No, I don't remember seeing you."

"What? That's impossible!"

"I'm telling you I don't remember."

"Maybe you were in some kind of a trance or something because you didn't have your medicine."

Anna started to walk away. "Man, you are really, really weird. I gotta go."

"Wait, how you gonna go? You don't have your scooter."

She spun back around and put her hands on her hips. "Oh, my God, you really have been spying on me. No, I didn't ride my scooter today."

"That's good because I don't think anyone over the age of 12 should be riding a scooter. You're very young- looking but I'm pretty sure you're over the age of 12."

Anna's eyes bulged and her mouth flew open. She took a deep breath. Jimmy stepped back. But what came exploding out of her mouth wasn't a rant or a rave or the string of curse words he was expecting but an insanely loud, raucous laugh that turned every head in the store in their direction. "Mister, I like you!" she sputtered. "You're not afraid to speak your mind. At least I like you right now. I can't say how I'll feel in the future about this little encounter because I have not been feeling quite right lately, but for now you're all right and I'm going to give you my phone number. It's my land phone. I may or may not answer and if I do I may refuse to speak with you. No promises. Don't call after 7. I go to bed early and before doing that I don't want to think about anything but what I can find decent to watch on Netflix." She gave him her number, nodded solemnly and turned and walked away for real this time, leaving Jimmy with his own open mouth from which, unlike Anna's, no sound came out at all.

CHAPTER EIGHTEEN

TONY

When Tony Bunson left Mendelssohn's poker game he went straight to his tavern in the East Village and began pumping down the Grey Goose. His staff knew better than to say anything like "Hey, Tony, you alright?" and the general decibel level in the crowded room fell a number of points as the patrons, mostly regulars, knew from experience to keep a low profile and be on high alert. As it turned out, however, Bunson's infamous temper failed to flare that evening and he was eventually driven home in an incapacitated state by Emilio Gonzalez, his veteran security guard, who deposited him in bed. This pattern was to continue for two weeks.

At the end of those two weeks Bunson was working the bar and just getting started on his evening drinking when John Camry walked in and sat down on a stool. "Whaddya say there big fella?" he said with a grin. Bunson emptied his shot glass and slapped it down on the counter.

"What the fuck do you want?" he barked. "Get the fuck out of my place." Snapping his fingers he summoned security.

John held up both hands as Emilio and his brother Joseph appeared immediately, flanking him on both sides. "Whoa, whoa, take it easy fellas, I come in peace, I'm an old friend of your boss, right Tony?"

Tony waved the men away with the back of his hand. "Alright, I'm gonna give this asshole a chance to explain himself before we throw him out. Just don't wander too far away."

Propping his elbows on the bar he leaned forward so far into John's face that his "old friend" felt compelled to hop off his stool.

"Jesus, Tony, take it easy," he whined, backing slowly away. "I'm just here to apologize for what went down at Mendelssohn's the other night. It was kind of partly my fault and I'm sorry I upset you."

"You're sorry you upset me. You're... sorry... you... upset me. That table had thousands of dollars on it and I was all set to win each and every fucking one of them but you had to go into some bullshit about which door you wanna go through when you die instead of playing the fucking game. You're sorry, John? Show me how sorry you are. Put your money where your mouth is. You got a few grand on you? 'Cause that's the only thing that's gonna keep me from calling the Gonzalez brothers back over here to throw you out on your ass." Filling and emptying his shot glass he slammed it down on the counter again. "Eh? Eh?"

John sat back down. "OK, listen to me, Tony. I know I fucked up and you have a right to be mad at me. I don't blame you a bit, I'd be mad too. But I have something for you that's gonna make you glad all that shit went down because otherwise I never would have considered giving it to you and you would have lost out on the opportunity. You're a very lucky man!"

"I'll be a very lucky man when I get my money," Tony snarled. He paused.

"Alright, what is it?"

"Have you got a back room?"

In the back was a poorly lit space not much bigger than a closet. They sat down on a shabby couch. Opening his backpack, John took out two pipes and handed one to Tony. Grabbing it from John's hand he held it up to the dim light, twisting his neck and turning the pipe ostentatiously every which way. "Gee, I don't see any gold or silver, I just can't help wondering how this piece of shit could be worth the thousands of dollars you owe me," he said with a menacing smile. He cocked his arm.

"Wait, Tony don't do that, don't throw it, these pipes are expensive. Anyhow, c'mon, man, it's not the pipe, it's what I'm gonna put in it and man it's gonna blow your mind. You wanna see gold and silver? You'll see that and pearls and rubies and shit you didn't even know existed." John pulled a plastic bag from his jeans pocket.

"Here, pass the pipe back a minute and I'll show you what I'm talkin' about."

"Drugs?" Tony barked." Hey, I don't do drugs. I drink. A lot. And I like it." He stood up. "So it's time for you to leave so I can get back to doing what I like."

"No, Tony, hold on, I'm not talking about pot or crack or horse or any of that shit, this stuff is the real deal, I'm telling you that if" - John groaned as Tony yanked him by the elbow and threw him off the couch onto the floor.

"What the fuck did I just tell you, motherfucker! I don't do drugs! Get outta here and don't come back unless you have the money 'cause if you come back without it I will feed you to the brothers and you will never walk again!"

Chapter Nineteen

ANOTHER DATE

After dialing Anna Jones's number for the third time and getting voicemail yet again Jimmy Hanson sat back in his tattered leather easy chair, lit a cigarette and resigned himself to failure. Well, he thought, she did warn me she might not pick up. He blew a smoke ring and attempted to send a stream through the bull's eye. No more ring. Time for some weed. The pipe he'd primed earlier with a pinch of potent sinsemilla began producing its effect only minutes after he toked and as he felt himself opening up he realized, She doesn't have my phone number so of course she's not answering, she thinks it's a robocall, I'm gonna have to leave a fucking message. Damn, I hate doing that, people never return calls. Shit! Oh, well, no choice. He dialed again.

"Hi, this is Anna, I can't answer your call right now but if you'll leave your name and number and a brief message I'll get right back to you as soon as I can."

"Hi, Anna, hope you're doing OK, uh, I was wondering if we could get together soon 'cause I'd really like to see you again. Uh, this is Jimmy, Jimmy Hanson, uh, you know,the guy who was lurking, uh, stalking, I mean watching, uh, I mean we met at CVS the other day and I just" -

"Ha ha, Jimmy you're so funny! I've been wondering if you would call or if you thought I was crazy or something but, like I said, I haven't been feeling quite right but now I feel better, so yeah, I'd like to get together, so whaddya wanna do? Jimmy? Jimmy? Are you still there?"

"Oh, sorry, I didn't expect you to pick up. Yeah, let's get together. Get some lunch maybe?"

"Sure, sounds good. You know the Lenox Saphire on Lenox at 127th?"

"Yeah, I've never been in but I know the place."

"Great, let's meet there. What day?"

"Doesn't matter to me, whenever you want."

"OK, how about tomorrow at say, 1pm?"

"Sounds like a plan. See you then!"

"OK, bye."

"Bye."

Jimmy took a deep breath and exhaled, took another hit on his pipe and exhaled again. This is too fucking much, he thought. I can't believe she's really going out with me. It's like that Joe Jackson song. But I'm not all that bad looking, am I? Really? He strode into the bathroom and looked in the mirror. All right, c'mon now, not all that bad, could be a little heavier, yes, a little on the short side, hair could be a little thicker and less gray, but good nose and mouth. Right? And anyhow it's less about looks with guys, they say. In all the interviews chicks always pick "he makes me laugh" as the number one trait they're looking for. Sure, there's gotta be some physical attraction but it's not that important and she said she thinks I'm funny. Nothing to worry about, it's gonna be great.

Feeling only slightly more confident he headed for the refrigerator for a Beck's.

***

At 12:55 the next day Jimmy was outside the Saphire chain- smoking Pall Malls.

He managed to get through three of them before Anna finally appeared.

"Hey, sorry I'm late."

"Nah, you're hardly late at all. And I got a chance to get my nicotine fix so I won't have to light up during the meal."

"Ha! Smoking's been banned in restaurants since practically the last century. You absolutely know that, man, who are you trying to kid?"

"I'm trying to kid you, kiddo. Anyhow, the weather's so nice we should just eat outside and then I could smoke."

"No, you still wouldn't be allowed to. And even if you were, you shouldn't do it 'cause you'd make everybody mad and you might get beat up."

"I'm still kidding by the way. And I wouldn't just get beat up. I'd probably get knifed or shot."

"Yeah, and I'd have to clean it all up."

"That would be very kind of you. Hey, I notice you didn't bring your scooter."

Anna smirked. "Very observant of you. I've been thinking maybe you're right that I'm a little too old to be riding a scooter."

"Ah, glad you're seeing it my way. You know, it isn't polite to ask a lady her age, but, uh, exactly how old are you?"

"That is indeed a rather impertinent question, sir, but since you ask, I'm just a sweet little sixteen."

They sat down. The waiter arrived suddenly with water and menus. Jimmy gulped from the first and hid behind the second. "Jimmy, what's wrong?" Anna laughed. "You didn't think you were going to have sex with me, did you? So there's no problem at all. We're just two new friends getting acquainted and having something to eat. What should we order? Look at all these Senegalese lamb dishes. I'm just super into lamb, how about you? I think I'll go with suppa kandja 'cause that has both lamb and fish and I just love fish. What're you gonna order, Jimmy? Hello-oh. Jimmy... C'mon, honey, don't be so discouraged, look at me. Put down the menu and look at me." Hearing the word "honey" Jimmy slowly lowered his menu and peeked over the top. "Oo hoo!" Anna chortled. "You look so pitiful, like a poor little puppy that's lost his mommy! Hey, man, don't you know when you're being teased? Do you really seriously think I could possibly be only sixteen years old? Look at these breasts!" Jimmy choked on his water and erupted in a long coughing fit which finally subsided with Anna patting him on the back with one hand and rubbing his chest with the other. She bent over close to his ear. "As for the sex," she whispered, "it's entirely dependent on your table manners. And I must say you're off to a terrible start so you'd better shape up, don't you think?"

CHAPTER TWENTY

SYNDY

"**W**here the hell have you been!" fumed Gunge shortly after John Camry put his lighter to his pipe. "You should be reporting back to me with a good deal more regularity. And I'm very disappointed in your fiasco with Bunson. You're going to have to do a hell of a lot better than that. You're going to have to figure out some way to bring him to me."

"Jesus," John moaned, "how do you know I went to see Bunson?"

"I simply inserted my request that you do so."

"Oh, that's right, you're constantly working on your abilities. But let me ask you. Do you have any idea what that guy is like? He's a goddamn savage brute, he's dangerous, he threatened to have his thugs turn me into a cripple if I so much as show my face again unless I give him a bunch of money that I don't even have and that I really don't even owe him, just because he's got this screwy idea I cost him the winning hand in a poker game and who knows for sure that he would have won it anyways."

"Are you about finished?"

"As a matter of fact, I'm not. For bringing you Anna you said you'd get me money and women. I haven't seen hide nor hair of either. I need women, or at least *a* woman, so I don't completely lose my mind and as for money, well I need it for myself but also I'm never going to get through to Bunson without it and where does that leave you, my fine, jolly little fellow?"

Gunge flashed one of his goofy, toothy grins. "You do have a point there, John, and I intend to do something for you very soon. I don't like to see my very best friend so unhappy. Just have a little more patience and I guarantee that in a short time you'll be very pleasantly surprised."

"Yeah, right, very best friend, " John muttered to himself as Gunge and his giant smile began to fade like the Cheshire cat.

***

"So Mr. Steely Dan is back," smirked John's nurse as she daubed his arm with alcohol. "Have you got a decent vein for me today or are you still shooting that heroin?"

"Oh wow, you actually remember me. Was it my snappy wit or my collapsed veins that impressed you so much?"

"I'm not sure 'impressed' would be really the right word."

"What would be the right word?"

"Curious?"

"OK, you can lower your eyebrows now."

The nurse laughed. "That's what I mean. You're kind of weird. I've met many oddballs but there's something about you that's just a half- step stranger than the usual."

"Hey, I'm not so weird, and I'm not really a heroin addict, you know, look at my arms - no tracks. Even that massive hemo whatever you call it you gave me last time has finally disappeared. My arms are smooth as silk. Besides, heroin sucks. I'll tell you what's fantastic. It's this shit called DMT that takes you to this place that's full of flashing lights and stuff and there's little people there that -"

"No, no way!" the nurse screamed and socked John in the shoulder. "I thought nobody knew about that drug except me and my brother. We've been doing it for years! Hey, That's it!

That's what's so eerie about you, I knew there was something, it's something to do with DMT but I don't know exactly what, it's like some kind of a premonition or something, I just don't quite know what it is. I just can't believe it!"

"What I can't believe is that I can't see you without experiencing some degree of pain, whether from a needle or an outright walloping," John groaned. "You really pack a good punch."

"Oh, I'm so sorry,"the nurse replied and was about to massage his shoulder but thought better of it. " I just got so excited to find another DMT fan!"

John smiled. "What's your name, anyways?"

"Syndy Lee."

"Well, Syndy, maybe we should put our pipes together and visit the land of the funny little men."

"Syndy smiled back."Maybe we should."

Chapter Twenty-One

A QUICK FLING

Jimmy managed to get his table manners together well enough that after the meal at the Saphire, to both his astonishment and anxiety, he found himself in Anna's one bedroom apartment in Washington Heights, surveying the walls crowded with bookcases and framed posters of Jimi Hendrix, the Who and the Beatles. "Well, you obviously didn't grow up with these guys so how'd you get turned on to them?" he asked. "Your folks?"

"Oh, man. The Beatles, the Stones, Dylan, the Beach Boys, they were always blasting them night and day. Sure beats the hell out of the crap coming out these days."

"You don't like rap?"

"Rap is crap. Hip-hop is pig slop."

"Yikes."

"Just 'cause it rhyme don't make it sublime."

"That could be a rap lyric right there."

Anna stuck her tongue out. "What would you like to hear? Rubber Soul, maybe?"

"Sounds good."

Anna smiled. "Yes, it will." She took the record out of its sleeve and put it on the turntable.

"Vinyl!" Jimmy crowed. "Haven't seen one of those in a while."

"There's no comparison. I hate digital shit. It's cold."

"I'm sure I don't really have the ears to hear the difference."

Handing him a joint Anna smiled again. "Here, try this. It's super good shit. You won't believe how good vinyl can sound."

By the time George Harrison's "Think For Yourself" came on they were in bed. When "Michelle" ended side one there was no question whether Anna was going to get up and flip the record, and their love making continued rhythmically in silence punctuated by moans, squeals and gasps until Jimmy ejaculated into Anna's hair. "Oh, my God," she groaned, "I have to see my dentist!"

Chapter Twenty-Two

THREE PIPES FULL

John was dismayed at Syndy's insistence that her brother join them at her Sunnyside, Queens apartment when they agreed, after some more casual flirtation at the hospital, on a time and day for what she called their "smoking date." "Don't worry," she chided, walking slowly around her living room. "Lee's great, I'm sure you'll like him. We always smoke together, it's just something we do. First it was pot, now it's DMT."

"Wait a minute. Lee? You call your brother by his last name?"

"No, that's his first name too."

"Lee Lee?"

Syndy nodded.

"Wow, that's so bizarre!"

Syndy shrugged. "Yep, that's what people say."

"Hey, I'm sorry. I didn't mean anything by it."

"That's all right, don't worry about it." The buzzer rang. "Here he is now."

Lee was tall and well-built like his sister and had the same jet- black hair but cut almost crew cut short. He extended a hand to John. "My sister's pretty particular about making new friends but she says you're into DMT, so that's a pretty good sign. Anyhow, I wanted to meet you and I've been itching to have a smoke so I figured I'd kill two birds with one stone. Or should I say while getting stoned?"

John laughed. "Nice to meet you. You two look pretty much alike and seem to be about the same age. You're not twins are you?"

"As a matter of fact we are," Syndy said. "Identical twins, no less. Even our parents have a hard time telling us apart."

John laughed again. "Gee, it's pretty easy for me. Maybe I'm not as dumb as I look."

"No," Syndy grinned, "that would be impossible."

***

After smoking they sat at the kitchen table drinking wine and eating bread and cheese. "'A jug of wine, a loaf of bread and thou,'" quoted John.

Syndy smacked her lips. "I guess poor Omar wasn't into cheese. He didn't know what he was missing."

Lee shook his head. "I see you're still having trouble controlling yourself at the table. But I have to admit this cheese is really great, so I'll forgive you."

"Oh, thank you, kind sir. It's extra extra sharp, that's what makes it so good. I can't stand bland cheese, it's like eating cardboard."

"What's that cheese that stinks so bad?" asked John.

"Limburger!" the twins answered in unison.

"Yeah, that's it. How can anybody eat that shit? And by shit I really mean shit. That's literally what it smells like."

Syndy pinched her nose. "Speaking of shit, now that we have some nourishment does anybody feel like talking about their trip, because I can't remember anything about it except I'm pretty sure there was a very bad smell."

"Well, you're doing better than me," Lee said. "I don't remember a bad smell because I don't remember anything. Things are always a little vague afterwards but this is the first time I'm drawing a total blank. It's kind of freaky. What about you, John?"

John took a sip of wine and cleared his throat. "Um, uh, yeah, it is kind of freaky. Maybe it's a weak batch of the drug or something."

"Can't be that," Lee replied. "It's from the same stash I smoked from a few days ago." Syndy shot him a look. "Hey, once in a while I smoke on my own, sis, there's nothing wrong with that. Sometimes I get a real hankering and you're not always available."

Syndy sighed. "Yeah, all right, that's OK, it's just that you're not in the best of health and I get concerned about you. It's my job, remember. I'm a nurse."

Lee stood up from the table and put on his jacket. "And don't think I don't appreciate the fact that you are concerned, but in general I'm doing a little better these days. Right now I'm feeling a little tired and burnt out, though, so I think I'll head home. Nice to meet you, John."

Lying in Syndy's bed that evening John turned his head to gaze at her sleeping form. I can't believe my good luck, he thought. Not only a beautiful woman but a nurse, someone to calm me and reassure me and take care of me when I get so scared there's something wrong with me and I don't know if I should see a doctor. Instead I can see a nurse, my own nurse who seems to really like me.

He closed his eyes, breathed in for four, held for four and breathed out for four but his guilty conscience would not let him sleep.

Chapter Twenty-Three

CURIOUS JOHN

When he got back home the next day John paid an early visit to Gunge, who was, as always, delighted to see him. "So soon, my friend!" he said with a smile. "Now that's what I like to see!"

John did not return the smile. "OK, cut the crap, Gunge. I wanna know what's going on. What the fuck are you up to?"

"Why, Mr. Camry, what can you possibly be so upset about? Didn't I promise you a girl? And such a beautiful oriental girl at that!"

"That's an insult and you know it. People don't say oriental anymore, they say Asian, moron!"

"You seem to forget I am not people, my friend. Otherwise you would not have your beautiful oriental Asian girlfriend. You have no reason to complain. I promised you a lover and I gave you one. Isn't she everything you always wanted in a woman? Good-looking, kind, uniquely able to take care of you and your many neuroses and hypochondrias?"

"I'm not complaining about Syndy. You're right, she's perfect, I'm amazed. But I know there's something tricky going on here. How come I can remember seeing you yesterday almost perfectly and Syndy and Lee remember nothing?"

"Because that's the way I want it."

"Why?"

"It's part of my plan."

"What plan? What are you up to? Why do you want me bringing you new smokers and what do you need old smokers like Syndy and Lee for?"

"I don't need Syndy except to keep my promise to you and Lee means nothing to me either. They're just two of thousands of visitors I tolerate but have no current need of."

"If they mean nothing to you why did you erase their memory? And what about Bunson? Why do you want me to bring him? What do you need him for?"

"You know, you ask a lot of questions. Now it's my turn. Do you know what the Big Bang is?"

"Of course I do."

"Well now, let me ask you this. How do you suppose your monstrous universe was only about the size of a pinhead 13 billion years ago and now it consists of enormous stars, black holes, dust clouds, galaxies, etc., all rushing at unfathomable speeds to incalculable distances? How could those uncountable tons of matter spread out over almost infinite space have once been contained in such a tiny space?"

"I don't know. Nobody does."

"It would be easier for you to understand that mystery than to understand me and my plans."

CHAPTER TWENTY-FOUR

JOHN SEES LEE

Having spent a good deal of time in high school, college, grad school and on his own trying to come to grips with the Big Bang Theory and given it up for a lost cause, John could only hope that Gunge was wrong. He decided to have a talk with Syndy's brother, who agreed to meet him at his Upper East Side apartment. Touring the living room Lee suddenly stopped, pursed his lips and turned to face John.

"You don't live alone, do you? This furniture, these knick- knacks, the curtains. There's a woman living here."

"Not any more, there isn't. My wife moved out. We're separated."

"Your wife! Motherfucker, you're dating my sister and you're married!?"

John, who on a good posture day might just graze 5'11" and after a full meal weigh 140 pounds, backed slowly away from his 6'2" guest. "Now wait a minute, Lee, just take it easy, we haven't had sexual relations in years and like I said she's moved out, we're not together anymore, we're not a couple we're not an item or anything like that, you know, it's like we're not really even married." His heels bounced against a stool and he collapsed backwards into his easy chair. Lee grabbed him by the shirt front and pulled.

"You better watch where you're going or you'll get into trouble," he said softly, lifting him out of the chair. "We wouldn't want that to happen now, would we?"

John adjusted his collar and ran his fingers through his hair. "No, I don't want any trouble, I swear I was gonna tell Syndy but I'm so afraid of losing her and she's really important to me, I really need her, man." He started backing away again, but more carefully. "You're not gonna hit me, are you?"

Lee laughed. "No, man, I'm not gonna hit you. You're too pitiful for that. And you do need a woman worse than anybody I ever saw, so I'm giving you a break. But you do anything to hurt my sister and the break I give you will be of your neck. For some reason she's crazy about you and I haven't seen her this happy in years and I'm not about to ruin that. Maybe against my better judgment." He let out a long slow breath and shrugged his shoulders. "God, I just hope I'm doing the right thing. Syndy's about the only thing I care about in this world. Most people love their brothers and sisters but I think maybe for twins it's even stronger." He shot John a look of both anger and worry. "I really mean it. Watch your step. I'm not a violent person but there are times when I have a very hard time controlling my temper. Know what I mean?"

"H-hey, man," John stuttered, "she's the most important person in my life, too. I swear I'm not bullshittin' you, I'd rather die than do anything to hurt her."

"Let's hope it doesn't come to that. Now, what did you want to see me about?"

"Would you like a beer or a smoke? I've got some dynamite weed that'll really set you on your ass. Two tokes and you're gone."

"No, I'm good."

"Well, I'm gonna have a little something to settle my nerves."

"Yeah, sure, sorry, maybe I overreacted a little. Knock yourself out."

John took a hit and held it in. "What kind of relationship do you have with Gunge?"

"What? I can't understand you. Blow that shit out and say it again."

John expelled a thick cloud. "What kind of relationship do you have with Gunge?"

"I still don't understand you. Who the hell is Gunge?"

Chapter Twenty-Five

ANNA SEES GENE

Anna opened the door to Dr. Mendelssohn's office, walked rapidly through the crowded waiting room, shot past the receptionist and went straight into where the doctor was working on an upper left molar. "Oh, Gene, I'm so sorry!" she burst out and began sobbing on his shoulder.

"Anna, what the hell!" he yelped, somehow pulling the drill out of his patient's mouth while only just barely grazing his cheek. "What the fuck's the matter with you? Can't you see I'm in the middle of something here? Hey, hey, baby what's wrong?" he whispered then, taking her face in his hands. "You're crying. What is it? C'mon, c'mon, I'm sorry I yelled at you, c'mon, sit down, sit down over here, let me just check on my patient a minute. Drink this."

Anna gulped the cup of water and ran to the door. "I'm sorry, I'm so sorry, I don't know what I'm doing," she moaned and was gone before Mendelssohn could stop her.

Chapter Twenty-Six

JIMMY SEES A SHRINK

Jimmy knew it was over after three days. Three days of incessant calling and always straight to voice mail, no callbacks, no texts, no emails, no anything. Yeah, fuck me, he thought. She told me this was gonna happen and guess what, it happened. Duh. I just knew it, I just fucking knew it was too good to be true. Shit! All right, all right, pull yourself together now, Jimmy boy, you'll always have the memories. Memories! Fuck that shit! I want that body in my hands, my dick in that pussy, my tongue down that throat! I can't do without it now that I've tasted it! He turned to his usual source of calm and inspiration, weed.

A few minutes later, as he lay spread-eagle and spaced-out on his bed it came to him. Yes! What's that chick's name? I know I have her card stashed away here somewhere. He found the card in the back of his underwear drawer: Dr. Sarah Smith, EdD, LCSW, Psychotherapist.

Within the week he was sitting on the couch in Dr. Smith's office on W. 137th Street. "I really like this leather couch, Dr. Smith. It's right out of Freud. Would it be OK if I lie down on it like I'm being psychoanalyzed by the illustrious doctor himself?"

"Whatever makes you comfortable, Jimmy. And I would be more comfortable if you'd just call me Miss Smith."

"Miss? No doctor?"

"Yes."

"Not Ms.?"

"No."

"Uh, OK. So, what should we talk about?"

"Why don't we start with what's bothering you the most There must be something bothering you or you wouldn't be here, right?"

"No, Doc, I'm doing just great. I heard you were really hot and I just wanted to check it out for myself."

Miss Smith crossed her legs and tilted her head back. "So am I?"

"What?"

"Am I hot?'

Jimmy stared at the rug. At the ceiling. At the walls. At the couch. Then he looked at Miss Smith. "I can't believe I said that and I can't believe you're not mad at me and yelling at me to get out. I'm horrible, I know, I'm sorry I said that. I'm really fucked up."

"What's wrong, Jimmy?"

"I lost my girlfriend. She's ghosting me."

"I see."

"Well, she isn't really my girlfriend, I guess. I've only known her a little while and we only got together once. She even warned me something like this might happen the first time we met."

"How did you meet her?"

"I saw her on the street and then I saw her again a couple weeks later and followed her into the drugstore."

"Is this something you usually do?"

"What?"

"Pick up women on the street."

Jimmy snickered and passed his hand across his forehead. "Wow," he said softly, stretching out full length on the couch. "I think I will just lie down here for a little while. I wasn't prepared for any soul searching or self-revelations. But I guess that's what this is all about, isn't it? Dig into the patient's psyche to see what makes him tick and drag out all the shit no matter how much it hurts. No, I don't pick up women on the street, I don't pick up women, period. That's what makes this so fucking painful. If I had a bunch of girlfriends it wouldn't be so bad but I do not have much luck with women and this one was like a dream come true. Of course I realized there had to be something fucked up about her because a beautiful young thing like that does not give her phone number to a middle-aged stranger the first time they meet without knowing a thing about him but I was not in a position to look a gift horse in the mouth. And now that I've had a taste everything's just worse than ever 'cause I know what I'm missing whereas before when I had nothing, it's like Dylan says, I had nothing to lose. Now I'm even more of a loser than ever." Jimmy bolted upright and screamed at the top of his lungs. "And it fucking sucks!"

Miss Smith stood and began walking slowly around the room. "Jimmy, you say she gave you her phone number, right? Tell me how that happened."

"I don't know," Jimmy replied, sitting forward on the couch, both hands wrapped around his head. "Of the many facets of my marvelous personality I somehow opted to go with the wise-ass and for some reason she seemed to find that amusing. Anyhow, like I said, there was definitely something not right with her and I'm sure she would have given her number to the hunchback of Notre Dame if he'd been there instead of me."

"Jimmy, that's the whole point. You were there. You chose to be there. You saw something you wanted, in this case an attractive woman, and you acted on it. You told me you never pick up women. Do you try?"

"No."

"You see! This time you tried! You made the effort and Jimmy, you were successful. Even if she had totally ignored you, you would have been successful because you made the effort, you had the courage to go for what you wanted."

"But I'm miserable."

"No, you think you're miserable but you're happy, Jimmy. Do you know why you're happy?" Jimmy took his hands from his head and shook it hard once to the left and once to the right. "You're happy because at last you put it all together. Didn't you say there was something wrong with her? That's why she doesn't call you back. It's not your fault she doesn't know what a good thing she had. You're better off without her, don't you see? Now you can move on and find someone who really deserves you, who you can have a real relationship with, not just a one -night stand. And you have no reason to be shy, you're an attractive man and now you know you have the nerve and daring to approach a woman you like and talk to her. I just wouldn't recommend doing it on the street."

Jimmy sat up straight, lifted his head, looked at Miss Smith and smiled.

CHAPTER TWENTY-SEVEN

BACK AT ANNA'S

Dr. Mendelssohn sat on the edge of the bed. Anna lay curled up beside him, her head just touching his side. "Anna, please, please, please tell me what's wrong. You haven't said a word since I came in twenty minutes ago. How can I help you if you won't tell me what's bothering you? I can't stand seeing you like this. What is it? Don't be afraid, just tell me. I just want to help you."

Anna reached for his hand and squeezed it hard. "I can't tell you Gene, I can't, I don't wanna hurt you and you'll never forgive me and you'll hate me for the rest of your life, I can't tell you."

Mendelssohn cradled her head and began rocking her gently back and forth. "Anna, Anna, don't you know me better than that?" he murmured. "I'm crazy about you, you've gotta know there's nothing you could say or do that would ever make me hate you. Whatever put that idea into your head? C'mon now, out with it. You know you'll feel better if you just tell me what's bothering you."

Anna removed her head from Mendelssohn's hands and put them in his lap. She looked at the door. "I wish I had a key to lock that door from the inside and then I'd swallow it so you couldn't run out when I tell you what happened." She took a deep breath and exclaimed in rapid fire, "I cheated on you Gene I'm sorry I don't know how it happened I really don't I don't know how it happened I didn't mean to are you happy now?" and burst into tears.

"Oh, my God!" Mendelssohn gasped," that's all? I thought you murdered someone!" He put his arms around her and pulled her to her feet, gently swaying, pressing her face to his chest. "Let's dance," he said and began to softly sing. "You are my sunshine, my only sunshine, you make me happy when skies are gray, you'll never know, dear, how much I love you, please don't take my sunshine away." While they slowly turned his shirt dampened with tears as Anna alternated between sobs and near hysterical laughter.

Chapter Twenty-Eight

JIMMY TRIES AGAIN

J immy made his way back to CVS, but not to hang out on Lenox Avenue smoking cigarettes. He went straight inside, threw a quick glance at the cashiers, picked up some Tylenol and got in line. Immediately, as he expected, a young black cashier fixed him with her gaze. Jesus, Jimmy thought, this girl really freaks me out. Every time I come in here she stares at me and I can't tell if she likes me or thinks I'm a weirdo who might do something dangerous. Jimmy and the girl had been involved in this little eyeballing relationship for months, long before he met Anna. Like her, she looked like a teenager and was cute, but nowhere near as attractive. Jimmy had figured out her schedule and would pick up a single item just to get the chance to have her ring him up. Although there were usually three or four cashiers, like a penny that consistently comes up heads it was almost always this girl who would be the one to call out, "Next guest" to him. He would slide his purchase across the counter, they would lock eyes, he would mumble, "How are you?" he would pay, she would hand him his change and purchase, they would lock eyes again, he would mumble, "Enjoy your day" and walk away. Which is exactly what happened again. "This is absurd," Jimmy grumbled under his breath as he walked back up Lenox. Frustrated and horny, he felt powerless as he realized how difficult it would be to ever get into any kind of a conversation with a cashier behind a counter and a line of customers behind him.

But the next day he got a break. Coming back from a walk up 125th Street and about to head home he thought he saw a familiar form in line at the Halal cart, but since he'd never seen his favorite cashier in street clothes he wasn't sure. "Let's go, man, have some guts, take a chance," he scolded himself and walked up to the girl, saw it was her and forced a nervous smile. "Hey, how you doing, you on your lunch break?" he asked. She was nervous too.

"No, no, I'm just about to go in, I haven't started work yet."

"Oh, you start at three. My name is Jimmy, by the way."

"I'm Awa."

"Yeah, I know."

"You know? How do you know my name?"

"From your name tag."

"I'm not wearing my name tag."

"No, from before. In the store."

"Oh."

Jimmy searched his brain for something to say. "Are you an artist, by any chance? A painter or a musician?"

"I don't know anything about art."

"You don't play the piano or the guitar or anything?"

"No."

"Oh, OK, I was just wondering. See you around."

"Are you an artist! I am the biggest fucking idiot in the whole fucking world!" he seethed as he stormed up the street to his apartment.

CHAPTER TWENTY-NINE

A VERY UNEXPECTED CALL

When John Camry answered his phone and heard the words, "Hello, John, this is Tony Bunson," he hung up, ran straight to the bathroom and threw up. He washed his face, went to the kitchen, took out a bottle of Jameson Triple Distilled Irish Whiskey, filled three shot glasses and had downed two of them before the phone ring again. "Fuck me!" he yelled. "Fuck me right in the fucking head!" He drank the third shot glass. "There's no way I'm gonna answer that fucking phone," he moaned. Then a vision of Tony breaking down his door and blowing away his stomach with a shotgun changed his mind. He ran to the living room and swiped frantically at the screen. "Shit shit shit!" he screamed as the call went dead. Then it rang again.

"Hello?"

"John, what's going on, I've been trying to reach you."

"T-t-tony? How'd you get my number?"

"Mendelssohn."

"Christ, why would he give you my phone number after what happened at the poker game?"

"Because I apologized to him, John, and I wanted to apologize to you."

"Tony, I don't know what you're up to but I don't have any money."

"I understand that, John, but I'm not asking for money. You came to me to apologize and I treated you like shit when it should have been me apologizing to you."

"Are you serious? Did you have a near-death experience and see the light? Or fall in with some Jesus freaks or something and get born again? Man, I don't buy it, last time I saw you, you threatened to have my legs broken."

"I've changed, John."

"You've changed. So you're gonna have my arms broken, not my legs."

"John, I'm serious. My wife left me. I can't see my kids."

"What's that got to do with me?"

"It's the drinking. It ruined my life. I'm trying to turn things around, so I quit."

"So?"

"So, I need your help, John. I know I've been a complete asshole to you and everybody else and I wouldn't blame you if you told me to go fuck myself, but I really do need your help."

"What do you want?"

"I've been drinking all my life. I quit cold turkey because I have to get my wife and kids back and that's the only way I'm gonna get 'em back. I know that. I also know I run a bar and that's a hell of a place to be when you're trying not to drink but I have a lot of will power and I know I can do it."

"Then what's the problem?"

"The problem is I gotta have something, man. I swore I'd never do drugs 'cause that was wrong, drinking was OK, that's what a real man does, but drugs were wrong. Well, I'm tellin' you I'm the kinda guy that's gotta have something, I'm climbing the walls, I'm bored out of my mind being straight all the time. So I'm willing to try whatever it is you brought me the other day. Will you help me? I'm begging you, John. Please."

"Christ, Tony, with the state you're in I don't think you're ready for what I originally had in mind. You should start out with some mellow weed and we can see how that goes and take it from there."

"Oh my God, John, thank you, thank you thank you!" Tony shouted. "Can you come by the tavern tonight? Anything you wanna drink, anything, whatever, everything's on me. In fact, if you help me get back with my family I swear it's free drinks for the rest of your life!"

"Hey, Tony, let's not get too far ahead of ourselves. I can turn you on but working out domestic problems is not exactly my field of expertise. I've had my own troubles in that department and things have not gone well."

"OK, OK, sure, I get it, sure. Uh, so can you come by tonight, man?"

"Why don't you come over to my place instead?"

"Your place? Uh, OK."

"Alone."

"OK."

"I'll text you the address."

John went back to the kitchen and refilled the shot glasses. He emptied them thinking, I am truly out of my fucking mind. Gunge, you stinking scumbag, I hope you're happy now.

CHAPTER THIRTY

AGAIN JIMMY TRIES AGAIN

Determined to put an end, one way or another, to the visual footsie games he'd been playing with Awa, Jimmy marched once more into CVS prepared to deal with her right across the counter, other customers be damned. To his great relief, a miracle had occurred. She was actually out on the floor helping a customer!

The second she was free he rushed up to her and blurted, "Hi, Awa, there's something I've been meaning to ask you for a while, would you like to have lunch with me one of these days?"

Awa looked like she'd just been given a diagnosis of terminal cancer. "No, I can't," she replied, edging slowly away.

"If not lunch, maybe coffee?" Jimmy persisted.

"No, I can't, I'm sorry," she said, retreating behind the counter and scurrying to her register.

From that point on, when Jimmy made his purchases Awa would rarely meet his gaze, and only for an instant.

CHAPTER THIRTY-ONE

ANNA AND GENE

For Dr. Mendelssohn and Anna Jones, on the other hand, things were completely different. They couldn't get enough of staring into each other's eyes, having sex, snuggling and just enjoying being together. The dentist closed his office for a week to spend time with the patient that mattered the most to him and they settled into a routine of being as lazy as possible for as long as possible until they felt an overwhelming need to go outside, where they would indulge in long, slow walks while holding hands, with frequent stops to look at each other and maybe kiss.

After coming in from one of these walks they sat down on the couch and Mendelssohn grabbed the remote. "How about another episode of Party Down?" he asked with a big smile.

Anna took his hand and gently removed the remote, setting it on the coffee table.

"Not yet," she said, "I'd like to get serious for a moment."

The doctor continued to smile. "Now what would you want to go and do a thing like that for? Just when we're having so much fun."

Anna passed her thumb across her lips, then did the same to Mendelssohn. "What's that all about?" he asked.

"Remember when we watched Breathless the other day? That's what Belmondo did."

"Yeah, a tribute to Humphrey Bogart, right?"

"I don't want us to be like Belmondo and Seberg in that movie."

"What do you mean?"

"No communication."

"What are you talking about? For the last three days we've spent almost every sleeping and waking minute together, laughing, having fun and talking, talking, talking."

"But not about what I did."

"I forgave you didn't I?"

"That's just it."

"What's just it? That I forgave you? You'd rather I didn't? You wanted me to say I never want to see you again?"

"Of course not."

"Then what? I don't get it. What are you complaining about?"

"I just wanna know how you could do it so easily."

"I told you. Everyone makes mistakes. You made a mistake. That's all. Period. Let it go."

Anna sighed. "It's just that if the situation was reversed I'm not sure I would be very nice about it. I love you too much. I know you love me but maybe you don't love me the way I love you." She paused. "And maybe that's why it's so easy for you to forgive me," she added, softly crying.

Mendelssohn cupped his hand over Anna's mouth. "Stop. Being. So. Foolish. How can you measure love?" He removed his hand and kissed her lips, then her eyes. "How do we even define love? Who really knows what love actually is? All I can tell you is that I've never felt this way about anyone before and nothing that you or anyone else does can ever change that. If you left me I would be devastated, but if that's what made you happy, I could accept it. I think. I don't know. Maybe I'd kill myself. Would that be enough proof for you that I love you?"

CHAPTER THIRTY-TWO

TONY AND JOHN GET HIGH

When Tony arrived at John's apartment, John was ready for him. He'd managed to steady his nerves to a reasonable degree of anxiety and apprehension by washing down an Ativan with a couple of Beck's and giving himself a pep talk consisting mainly of the mantra, "Tony doesn't want to hurt me, he's hurting his own self and needs my help" repeated dozens of times. But he did jump when the buzzer rang.

Opening the door he forced himself to be jovial. "Welcome aboard, sir, we run a taut ship, we'll brook no nonsense."

Tony frowned. "What? What do you mean, I don't understand."

"Hey, I'm just joking with you. Come on in and relax. I'd offer you a beer but I guess that would be a bad idea. How about a Coke or 7-Up maybe?"

Tony took off his hat and laid it gently next to him on the couch. "Could I just have a glass of water, please?"

"Sure, sure, coming right up."

In the kitchen John began a new mantra under his breath. "You're doing great, you're doing great, everything's cool, everything's great."

"Man," he said, walking back into the living room and handing Tony the water, "if anybody back at Mendelssohn's was taking bets on you and me getting together like this after what happened he'd have made a fortune."

Tony coughed and took a sip of water. "Yeah, uh, I'd really rather try to forget about that poker game. I'm not too proud of it."

"Of course, sorry, man, it was stupid of me to bring it up. The whole point of why you're here is to move beyond that, to get you to a better place, and I've got just the thing for it." John sat back in his easy chair, crossed his legs and laughed. "You know, I still remember perfectly the first time I got high. It was back in college, at Dartmouth. All the hip kids had been smoking for months and I really wanted to but there was so much bullshit coming down from adults about how harmful pot was that I was just too damned scared to try it. Finally, I decided I was ready to take a chance. My two best friends came to my little dorm room with the Hair album and a little block of hashish. 'The object of tonight,' they said, 'is to get John high.'" John stood and walked to the window. "Well, I'm afraid I did not get high. At least not at first. Not until we walked across campus to another dorm where some of our friends were smoking on the second floor and I happened to look out the window. 'The night is so black,' I said to no one in particular and from the way the letter "l" in the word "black" sounded when I said that I realized I was finally feeling something. Not much, but something." Returning to his chair he raised his hands palms out to Tony. "The reason I'm telling you all this is to let you know beforehand that a lot of people don't feel much the first time they smoke and I don't want you to feel disappointed if that happens to you."

Tony nodded. "Let's do it."

Chapter Thirty-Three

TONY MEETS GUNGE

Not only did Tony have no problem getting high on John's pot, he enjoyed it so much he insisted they go straight to the next step. "OK, man, this is good, really good, I like this feeling, I'm ready for that shit you were gonna give me back at the tavern,"he declared as John took a deep breath in relief and clapped his new friend on the back.

"I'm so glad to hear that, Tony, weed is so much better for you than alcohol and it's going to give you some really good insights into your situation and lots of new ideas on how to make things better." He paused. "But maybe we should take it slow. I can give you some to take home with you and you can use it to mellow out for a few days and then we can look into trying DMT."

"DMT? Is that the stuff you were talking about?"

"Yeah."

"What does that stand for?"

"Dimethyl something or other, I don't remember the full name. But I really think we should wait on it, it's pretty powerful stuff and now that I think about it I'm not sure you really need it. You'll do fine with the pot, that's a nice calm high and you can always try the DMT down the line sometime."

"Now, wait a minute,wait a minute, man, I wanna hear more about this DMT. What does it do?"

John sighed. "Have you ever heard of ayahuasca?"

"No."

"Well, it's this psychedelic brew that the Amazon Indians use to get super high and one of the ingredients is DMT. You drink it and get sick but then have these incredible visions and experiences. But we wouldn't be doing that, we just smoke the DMT and you don't get sick but you do have some far out hallucinations, like I told you before. At least I think they're hallucinations, nobody really knows what they are and they're completely real when you're having them. You see all these jewels and little people and stuff."

"Shit, man, c'mon, I'm ready for that! I wanna see that shit!"

John got up and headed for the kitchen, calling back over his shoulder, "Sure, but whaddaya say we have a drink first? Oh, fuck, I forgot you're not drinking. Sorry, I just keep forgetting!"

Fuckin' hell! he thought. He leaned on the kitchen counter and poured himself a shot of whiskey. If I don't do what he says, he could turn back into the old Tony and then I've had it. But if the DMT doesn't go well there's no telling what he might do. Fuck me! He gulped the shot. "Into the valley of Death rode the 600..." With an exaggerated smile he jogged back into the living room. "OK, Tony!" he shouted. "Let's rock and roll!"

Tony took the pipe John offered and stuck it in his mouth. "Light me up," he snarled and minutes later he and Gunge were the best of pals.

Chapter Thirty-Four

TONY IS REINSTATED

When Bill and Bob Pletz walked into Dr. Mendelssohn's living room and spotted Tony Bunson sitting on the couch they looked at each other and high- fived. "Whoa!" they shouted simultaneously. Bob walked over to shake Tony's hand. "The gold medal winner in the Olympic card table toss!" he laughed. "I heard about what happened. I never expected you'd be invited back here ever again!"

Tony smiled. "Well, we're not playing poker, the doc says we're not quite ready for that. This is kind of a trial to see if I can get along with everyone after what happened last time."

The buzzer rang and the regular poker crowd strolled in - Mendelssohn's cousin Charles, Jack French and John Camry, who'd given them a ride. When everyone was seated, Mendelssohn stood up and cleared his throat.

"Ahem, my dear friends," he said in a deep, dramatic voice, then paused for the chuckling to subside. "I'm sure you're wondering what Tony is doing here in light of what went down the last time we got together for poker." Tony put his hands in his pockets and studied his shoes. "I know I promised there was no chance Tony would ever be invited back here and when I said that I meant it, but things have changed, and Tony has changed. He has apologized to me and has convinced me that he is on the path toward becoming a new and better person and I think we should give him a chance. But I do ask you, Tony, to now apologize to your friends here as sincerely as you did to me."

Tony slowly stood and put his hands awkwardly behind his back. "My dear friends," he began in perfect imitation of Dr. Mendelssohn, which caused general tittering and a howl from Bob Pletz. Tony forced a shy smile. "Phew, maybe you're not as mad at me as I thought you would be and that's a big relief because I wasn't sure I wanted to come here and face you all. It's hard to face the fact that you've been a piece of shit and acted like an asshole, especially to good people like you. All I can say is I'm really and truly sorry and like the doc said I'm doing my best to turn myself around and I hope you'll forgive me and give me another chance. Thank you!"

Tony sat down to a smattering of applause and Dr. Mendelssohn stood up again. "I'm glad you all feel as I do, that everyone needs a break now and then and especially Tony, who's been going through some very hard times. And now I'd like to present you with another surprise guest, one who, if I don't miss my guess, will be even more to your liking." Turning to the left, he stretched out his arms. "Gentlemen, I give you my girlfriend, the lovely Anna!"

With her hair piled on her head and wearing a low-cut red dress, Anna sashayed out from the bedroom with a model's runway walk and paraded slowly around the living room. The Pletz brothers high-fived again. Anna stopped walking and put her hands on her hips. "One or two of you,"she began, "may feel that with this little charade I'm setting women's rights, which seem to be making a little more progress lately, well, that I'm setting them back 60 or 70 years, back to when the swimsuit competition at the Miss America contest was a must- see, when Playboy Magazine was a must- read for all one hundred percent red-blooded American men. And you'd be right! But this was all my idea, Gene tried to talk me out of it, he was dead set against it." Anna walked over to Mendelssohn and took his hand. "But I did a little sweet talking and changed his mind for him," she fake whispered in a loud voice.

Mendelssohn shook his head and shrugged his shoulders. "She can be pretty persuasive," he admitted, "but to tell you the truth I still don't really understand her motivations. I don't understand her at all. I only know that I love her very much."

Still hand in hand, they both bowed, and to calls of "Kiss! Kiss!" turned to face each other and complied. "All right, now that that's been taken care of," the doctor shouted over the loud reaction from his guests, "Charles, would you please pass out the pipes so we can return to Magicland!"

Chapter Thirty-Five

TONY AND GUNGE

"Tony, my boy, so good to see you again!" Gunge howled, simultaneously turning cartwheels, changing size and juggling diamonds, rubies and sapphires.

"I'll never get used to it!" Tony gasped, futilely extending his hands toward the jewels. "How the fuck do you do that? Is anything real here? I can't fucking understand it!"

"Don't try to understand, my friend, just enjoy," Gunge replied. "You had a good time your first visit, didn't you?" Tony nodded. "Now that's what counts, my very good friend, that's what counts. After all, your life has been very difficult lately and you deserve to have a good time. I'm going to see to it that you have plenty of good times from now on. How does that sound, Tony?"

Tony smiled. "That sounds pretty damn good to me." Then he frowned. "But what exactly do you mean by good times from now on and why are you doing anything at all for me? You don't even know me. And what do you get out of helping me, anyway? If there's one thing I know about this fucked- up world it's that nobody does anything for anybody without wanting something in return."

"Oh, Tony," Gunge replied with a shake of his head, "such cynicism in one so young! You're only 40 years old and yet you talk like a bitter old man. This is why you have such sadness in what you call your 'fucked- up world.' You must learn to trust and then you'll see how things begin to flow your way, that your world is a good world and life in it is beautiful and worth living. I want nothing from you for myself, I just want to see you happy, that will be reward enough for me for the things I will do for you."

"What things?" Tony shouted. "How can you do anything for me in my world? I don't even know who you are or what this place is! Is this another world or are you in my head or what?"

"Just shut up!" Gunge screamed. "All you need to know is that I'm going to do things for you! That's all you fucking need to know! You don't need to know what those things are, just that I'm going to do them. So stop with your stupid- ass questions and enjoy what I do for you!"

Chapter Thirty-Six

ANNA SLIPS AGAIN

Anna woke up with a heavy head. She looked at her watch. 9:37. She looked at the unfamiliar walls and pulled back the sheets. She was naked. So was Tony, who walked in from the bathroom toweling his hair. "Hey, baby, how you feelin'?" he called out with a grin.

"Oh my God!" Anna screamed, scrambling for her clothes, which lay in a pile at the base of the bed. "What the fuck am I doing here!" She kneed Tony in the groin and he fell to the floor with a loud groan. She jumped into her jeans, threw on her blouse and one shoe and kicked him in the head with it. "You fucking asshole!" She kicked him again. "You fucking asshole!" She kicked him once more and ran to the door. "You stinking fucking piece of shit!" She stumbled bawling down the hotel hallway with one shoe on, holding the other in her hand, trying without success to slip it on without stopping. Tony, writhing on the bedroom floor in pain, was also bawling.

When she got home Anna found that the phone she'd been so frantically searching for on the subway was lying on her bed. She called Dr. Mendelssohn. He was in the middle of an intricate procedure she was told and would call her back. She carried her scooter down to the street and rode it up and down Lenox Avenue for an hour, carried it back upstairs, took a handful of Ativan and lay down on the bed sucking her thumb.

CHAPTER THIRTY-SEVEN

PLETZ

"Hey, Bill!" Bob, spraying cracker crumbs, called out from the living room to his brother in the kitchen, "we got any bars of candy?"

Bill dropped the knife he was chopping radishes with, speared his way through the bead curtain separating the kitchen and living room and stood in front of Bob with his arms folded. "Bars of candy? What the fuck, man? Is that another of your British expressions, like torch? You do mean candy bars, right?"

"Yeah, I just like the way it sounds."

"Well, it sounds pretty stupid if you ask me."

"Nobody asked you."

"That's good because I get asked a lot of stupid things, you know what I mean? Hey, did you hear what happened to Doc Mendelssohn's girlfriend?"

"That hot chick we met at his house who was wiggling her ass all over the place?"

"Yeah, that's the one."

"What happened? Somebody rape her?"

"Jesus, bro, what's the matter with you?"

"Well, she's awful flirty, and you know what that can lead to."

"She OD'd. The doc found her just in time and now she's in a coma."

"Holy shit! You think we should go see her?"

"What good would that do? She isn't awake, she wouldn't even know we're there. But maybe we should pay a visit to the doc and offer our support. He must be really hurting."

"Yeah, that's a good idea, maybe he'll set us up with a couple hits of the old nitrous!"

When they arrived at Mendelssohn's house he was just putting the key in the door. "Hey, Doc," Bill called out as he and Bob hurried up to the front porch. "How's your girl, how's she doing?"

"Hi, boys, it's good to see you," he replied. "She's still in a coma, there's no change. Come inside, please come in."

They walked slowly into the living room. Mendelssohn gestured toward the couch. "Have a seat. Beer?" They nodded. "Budweiser or Beck's?"

"Budweiser?" Bob snorted. "Might as well drink piss."

"I believe," Bill said loudly, turning angrily toward his brother, "Budweiser was none other than Paul Newman's favorite beverage. Shit, man," he whispered, "give the guy a fucking break!"

"I think you're right about that, Bill,"Mendelssohn called out from the kitchen, "but I have to agree with your brother. I just keep Bud on hand for anyone who might happen to like it, but I can't stand it either. Let's go with the Beck's all around. Unless you do prefer Budweiser, Bill."

"No, man, Beck's all around, like you say."

Mendelssohn passed him a glass and he cleared his throat. "A toast. To your lovely lady, that she gets well soon." They clinked glasses.

"And to you boys, for coming over. I appreciate that," added Mendelssohn.

Bob wiped foam from his mouth with the back of his hand. "We probably should have called first, but we had a feeling you would be here and we were tired of sittin' around." He pulled a joint from the pocket of his frayed denim shirt. "Mind if we smoke?"

Mendelssohn smiled." I think that's exactly what I need. And I still have a full tank in the back. I'll fill some balloons."

Bob turned to Bill with a big grin, nodded his head vigorously and pumped both thumbs up and down.

Chapter Thirty-Eight

JOHN CONFRONTS GUNGE

John barely had time to put down his pipe before Gunge loomed into view, his face distorted in a broad smile that concealed a grimace. "Johnny, my boy, how the hell are you?" he leered. "Come to see your old pal again, have you?"

"Yeah, pal," John drawled, "I've come to see you again. I'd like some answers."

"If you'd like some answers that must mean you have some questions, and as you know I'm always here at your beck and call to help you in any way I can to navigate your troubled world."

"That's so very sweet of you, pal. I knew I could rely on you. I know you have only my interests at heart. You know how I know?" Gunge cocked his head to the side and wiggled his red eyebrows. "I know this because of all the visitors you get I'm the only one who seems to get anything out of our meetings. Nobody else remembers diddlysquat of what went on when they leave your divine presence, and one in particular, who you particularly wanted me to introduce you to, has been having a very bad time of things lately. Perhaps you may remember her, a young lady who goes by the name of Anna Jones?"

"Ah, yes, Miss Anna Jones, I do remember her. What seems to be the problem?"

"I don't know how much you know of what goes on in what you call our troubled world so I'll just tell you that she happens to be in a coma."

"A coma, you say. And just how did that coma bout?"

John stared for along time at Gunge's obsidian eyes. "You really have no heart, do you?" he finally said. "No heart at all."

"And just what do you call this?" Gunge replied, his heart bursting with a loud crack from his chest, expanding and contracting violently like Jim Carrey's in The Mask. With each outward pulse it grew bigger until it split the room's jeweled walls, which took on the dimensions and contents of Dr. Mendelssohn's living room.

"Holy shit!" John yelled. "That's Mendelssohn's place!"

"Very observant," Gunge commented, though he was nowhere to be seen. "Now take another look."

"It's us when we last got together - me and Mendelssohn, Charles, Tony Bunson, Anna..."

"And don't forget those lovely orphans, the Pletz boys," added Gunge. "They really are something, aren't they? It's so wonderful that the doctor continues to look out for them even though they are a couple of real good-for-nothings."

"Look who's talking."

"Still so bitter about life, John? It must be your general pessimism that drives you to attack me, your selfless benefactor. Do you forget that you were alone, you had no one, I promised you someone and now you have Syndy, the girl of your dreams? Have you forgotten that, John, my ungrateful friend?"

'Yeah, Gunge, I am an ingrate, I'll grant you that. I don't count my blessings, blessings I only half enjoy because it's never enough, I always want more and I can't help it, there's nothing I can do to change the way I am. But you, you're even worse, there's something about you that's very very bad, even if I can't quite put my finger on it. Just plain very very bad. Or maybe we could use the word evil. Yeah, evil, that pretty much captures it. Very very evil."

Chapter Thirty-Nine

Bellevue

"OK, we stay on the L until Union Square and then we get the 6," Bill Pletz advised Bob as they got on the subway. "Just in case I fall asleep."

"You won't fall asleep," Bob remarked, "not if I have anything to do with it."

"What's that supposed to mean?"

"Nothing. I got things to talk about, that's all, so I don't want you to go to sleep on me."

"Things? Like what?"

"Like Anna. She is so fucking hot, man! Look, there's a couple of seats over there."

They sat down and Bill turned to his brother. "She's in a coma," he whispered dramatically. "We're not going to the hospital to ogle her. We're going because the doc says when people talk to people who are in a coma they may be listening even if they don't react and it can help them to wake up. Got it?"

"Yeah, Bill, I get it but I'm still looking forward to seeing how hot she is, even if we won't be able to see her body 'cause she'll be under a sheet."

"You're just incorrigible, bro."

"In corri-what?"

"Never mind. Don't ever change. I love you just the way you are."

"That's good 'cause I don't like it when things change, especially people. Hey, you see those two Black guys sitting down there in the corner?"

"Yeah, what about 'em?"

"They're really lucky, aren't they?"

"Lucky? What makes them lucky?"

"Well, I mean they get all the chicks 'cause they got really big dicks."

"What the fuck, man? Where you comin' from with that shit? You going gay on me now?"

"No, man, I'm just sayin'. I seen it on the internet. Don't try to tell me you don't watch PornHub, I know you watch that shit too."

"Jesus, bro, that's porn, all the guys have big dicks. That's how they get the job."

"Well, maybe, but the Black guys are bigger."

"I don't know, I think I read somewhere that's not really true, studies have been done to disprove that myth."

"Oh, yeah? Well, then I'll tell you who's gay, bro, the guys doing those studies."

Bill stifled a laugh. "OK, Bob, good one, you got me that time. But Christ, man, you're missing the whole picture. 400 years of oppression and you see nothing but a racial stereotype. Those guys are far from lucky. Lincoln may have freed the slaves over a hundred years ago but Black people are still being treated like second class citizens. Still, man, still! A cop could come into this car at the next stop and arrest those cats for nothing, just because they're Black."

"But-"

"No, don't but me, man, it's true. That shit actually happens. Don't you read the papers or watch the news? It's even getting worse instead of better."

"Hey, bro, give me a break, I didn't sign up for a fucking history lesson."

"All right, all right, I'm sorry, I know you didn't mean any harm with your ridiculous comment and I'll shut up in a minute. But look. You know who Chris Rock is, right?"

"Hey, I'm not a moron."

"OK. I know you're not. I just wanna make one final point and then I'll shut up. Chris Rock said there's no white man in the world who would want to trade places with him and that's because he's Black. The motherfucker is bang ass rich and famous but still no white man wants to be him!"

"Sheesh! Hey, isn't this Union Square?"

***

At Bellevue Bob sat down at the foot of Anna's bed and Bill took a seat facing him. "Anna, how are you?" Bob called out. "It's me, Bob, and my brother Bill. I know you don't know us very well but we met at the doc's place the other day and we wanted to come see how you were doing." To Bill he whispered, "She's looking really good!"

"Jesus," Bill whispered back, "try not to say anything stupid, OK? Remember, even though she's in a real deep sleep, she might be able to hear you."

"Well, what should I say then? Should we talk about the weather? Hey, Anna," he said with a loud voice, turning toward her and advancing on his knees up the bed, "you're lucky to be in this nice air conditioned room, it's really hot outside."

Bill jumped up and grabbed his arm. "Get off the fucking bed you fucking idiot!" he growled through his teeth, pulling him almost to the floor. "Jesus H. Christ, don't you have any sense at all?"

"Let go, man, that hurts!" Bob yelled, twisting and shaking his arm to break away from Bill's grasp.

"Alright, alright,"Bill shushed, releasing him and straightening his shirt with soft pats. "I'm sorry, Bob, I'm sorry, but just quiet down now or we're gonna get thrown out of here. Oh, no, too late."

A tall, broad-shouldered female nurse had silently entered the room and was standing in the doorway with hands on hips. "Would it be too much if I was to remind you fine gents that this is a hospital," she said in a light Irish brogue, "and not a roller darby or a discotheque?"

Bill put his hands together as if in prayer, and stooping slightly shuffled slowly toward her until only a small gap was left between them. "Madame," he said with a gentle bow of the head, "can you ever forgive us? You see my poor brother here." He made a sweeping gesture to where Bob was standing stiffly near the far wall. "He was quite taken aback to see the dire condition into which his dear friend and classmate has so suddenly fallen. I'm afraid he simply lost control of his strong emotions and in his weakened state allowed his pent-up grief to burst forth from within. I can assure you this will not happen again and once more do beg your mercy in this very trying circumstance."

The nurse folded her arms, pursed and then unpursed her lips, unfolded her arms and sighed. "I see you boys are sincere in your concern for the poor young lady's welfare. I will allow you to stay and commiserate for now, but if I hear one more peep of ruckus coming from this room I will personally throw the both of you out on your ears." She pivoted in the doorframe and was gone.

"Oh, man, I thought she'd never leave," laughed Bob, pulling a vape pen from his jeans pocket. "But she was kinda fun and this will be even funner."

"What the fuck, Bob, you can't smoke that thing in here!" Bill hissed. "You wanna get thrown out on your ear like the nurse said? And maybe arrested too?"

"Hey, man, this is the top shit. I got it from my man Chico in the Village. Just one toke and you're flyin',you're wailin', Jennings. Nobody's gonna smell diddly from just one toke. We can blow it under the bed. Maybe it'll wake up the girl."

Bill chuckled. "It's impossible to stay mad at you. Wailin' Jennings. You didn't make that up yourself did you?"

"Nah, that's what Chico says. He's got a lot of different ways to get you to buy his shit. But all he's gotta say is it's good and I'm on it. It's always the best."

"All right, but I'll pass. At least one of us has gotta have his head on straight. Hurry up, we should get that talking thing going and get the hell out of here."

Bob took a toke and held his breath. "OK, what should we talk about? Not the weather, right?" He put his head under the bed and exhaled slowly. "Yipes! This stuff is strong! You gotta try this shit when we get home, man."

"Yeah, I will. Listen, I have an idea. Let's talk about the shit we used to do when we were workin' at J&R. That was some good fun. Not the actual work, but making fun of people. Maybe Anna will get a kick out of it if she can hear us. Let's get up close to her so we don't have to talk too loud. Remember when we were out of stock on something and somebody would ask if we had any in the back? Remember that one?"

"Yeah! You'd flap your hands around on your back and say, 'Nope, nothing in the back.' That was a good one! Or how about when something was on sale but it was sold out and they'd say, 'Can I get a raincheck?' and we'd run to the front of the store and come back and say, 'It's a little cloudy but it don't really look like it's gonna rain.'"

"Alright, another good one, I forgot about that one! But here's my favorite. You'd be working the cash register and you ring it up and the girl says she doesn't need a bag. But as she's walking away you say just soft enough so she can't quite hear, 'Oh, yes you do, to put over your head so nobody has to see your ugly face.'"

"Oh shit!" Bob started laughing. "One time you said it too loud and the girl heard you! She got so fucking mad! Oh, man, you remember that, Bill? It was so fucking hilarious!"

He started walking around the room, jumping up and down. "I can't stand it! It was just so funny her expression, man! You got in so much trouble with that shit!" His eyes were watering and he began to cough uncontrollably. "I just can't stand it!"

"Shut the fuck up! That nurse is gonna come back and we'll be in a hundred times worse trouble than that was. C'mon, let's get outta here! Now!"

Bob took a deep breath. "OK, but I just gotta say goodbye to Anna. Hey, I think her eyelids are fluttering!"

Chapter Forty

ANOTHER GET-TOGETHER AT MENDELSSOHN'S

The same crowd as last time was at Dr. Mendelssohn's: the Pletz brothers, Cousin Charles, Jack French, John Camry and Tony Bunson. But this time John's friends, Syndy and Lee Lee were also present. Once again, the doctor stood up to address his guests.

"I'd like to thank you all for coming. John's friends Syndy and her brother Lee are graciously joining us this evening and I trust you will all make them feel welcome. Now, to the news. I have some good news and some bad news. The bad news is that Anna will not be doing any modeling for us the way she did last time. The good news is that she is out of her coma and resting in good health in the back." A cheer went up and glasses were clinked. "The hospital called to tell me that when they went to check again on two young men who were getting rowdy in Anna's room the men were gone but Anna was awake and sitting up in bed with her eyes open and a smile on her face. Now, I'm not sure but I think I have a pretty good idea of who those two young men might have been..."

"Us!" howled Bob,raising his bottle. "Me and Bill!"

Mendelssohn laughed and began clapping his hands to a slow beat. "That's right, Bob, you and Bill!"he shouted. Charles and John added their hands, Mendelssohn began to sing "You Are My Sunshine" and soon everyone was clapping and singing along, most of them, the doctor included, in tears. Eventually, he raised his hand for silence.

"I don't have to tell you how much this means to me, boys, and Anna and I will never forget that you were instrumental in her recovery. At least, I will never forget. Another bit of bad news is that although she is awake and seems healthy and is eating and sleeping normally, Anna is not speaking and appears to be in a state of shock. She does not respond to questions, whether spoken or written down. We have no idea of what she knows or remembers, of why she overdosed or how long it will be before she returns to normal and can tell us what happened to cause her to take those pills. What we do know is that physically, as I said, she is doing well and her doctors have good hopes that she will fully recover. Now," he added, taking a seat, "there is something I would like to try. We are all well-versed in the use of drugs for both recreational and learning purposes. John has mentioned that Syndy and Lee have no recollection of what goes on in their latest

DMT trips, yet he is acutely aware of exactly what transpires in his. I asked him not to share any information, however, until we carry out this little experiment I propose. Are you all familiar with lucid dreams?"

"Sure," volunteered Charles, "but I wish I were more familiar with them than I am and had more of them than I do. They're absolutely fantastic! It's when you're aware that you're dreaming and can do anything you want. Travel all over the world or the universe, have sex with Marilyn Monroe, hit a home run at Yankee Stadium. And the best part of it is they're so incredibly real, more real than reality itself!"

Mendelssohn lit a cigarette. "Well, cousin, you're one of the lucky ones. The closest I've ever come is to realize I'm dreaming but then wake up before I can hit that home run. At any rate, it's not lucid dreaming I'm proposing but a little trick that lucid dreamers employ to help bring those dreams about. Supposedly, if you study your hands during the course of the day then you might find yourself doing that same thing in your dreams and that would trigger an awareness that you are in fact dreaming. So what I'm suggesting is that we give that a try before we smoke and see if it will make us cognizant during the trip that we need to try to remember what's happening when we come down. Now, of course, looking at our hands right now just before we smoke is probably not going to have much effect, but if we make a habit of it maybe when you smoke on your own in the coming days something will happen. So, before we light up, can I see a show of those hands we'll be studying from all those interested in trying this little experiment?"

Every hand went up.

CHAPTER FORTY-ONE

JIMMY SEES MISS SMITH AGAIN

After weeks of smoking pot, listening to music, bingeing Netflix and finding Awa the cashier at CVS as cold as ever, Jimmy Hanson decided his only hope was making another appointment with his shrink, who had at least made him feel a little better about himself the last time he was so depressed.

"Hi, Jimmy, so good to see you again," she said, extending her hand. "It's been a while and I wondered how you were doing."

"Not so hot," he murmured, heading straight for the leather couch.

"What's wrong? More woman trouble? More problems with your ghostly girlfriend?"

"No, I gave up on her. Anyhow, like I told you, she wasn't really my girlfriend. We only got together once. But after I saw you, a little confidence returned and I decided to try to get something going with this cashier who'd been giving me the eye, but that fell through too."

"What happened?"

"I asked her out and she said no. As simple as that."

"Jimmy, I think maybe you're not meeting the right kind of woman for you. A cashier, a girl you saw on the street. My guess is that you would do better with someone with a more professional background, someone who would understand you better."

"What's wrong with being a cashier? I've worked as a cashier."

"What do you do for a living now, Jimmy?"

"I'm retired. I used to be in software."

"You see, that's what I'm talking about! You're an intelligent man and you should be setting your sights higher. There's something I'd like to try with you that I think would be very helpful." Miss Smith pulled open a desk drawer. "Do you smoke pot?"

Jimmy snickered. "That's about all I've been doing for the past three weeks."

"Alright, good. What about nitrous oxide?"

"What's that? Oh, yeah, you mean laughing gas, right. Haven't had it in a long time. None of the dentists I go to use it any more. I swear they're all fuckin' sadists, they get off on causing pain."

"Well, Jimmy, I guarantee I will not cause you any pain. Far from it." She passed him a pipe and a small, orange prescription bottle. "Put just a pinch in the bowl and smoke it." She stood, adjusted her skirt and strode off toward a door in the back of the room. "I'll be back in a second."

She returned with two inflated red balloons. "I don't think you'll need them both, but just in case. How are you feeling?"

"Yeah, that's good herb. I'm feeling it already. So, what's with the balloons? Just suck 'em down?"

Miss Smith put one up to his mouth. "Now just open wide and when I say 'Go' take a deep breath and hold it like it was smoke. Ready, set, go!"

When Jimmy came back down to earth less than a minute later he was ecstatic. "That was the best thing ever! I felt like everything was perfect. Everything in this whole fucked up world is actually exactly the way it's supposed to be, there's nothing wrong, it's all happening the way it was destined to happen since the beginning of time! And it seemed like I could hear everything, I could hear my heart and my breath and I heard someone singing, singing beautifully! Was that you? Were you singing?"

"Yes, Jimmy, that was me," Miss Smith answered, unbuttoning her blouse. "I was singing an old song from my childhood, one we learned in school, 'You Are My Sunshine.' Did you know it was written by the governor of Louisiana, Jimmie Davis? A Jimmy just like you." She pulled out her left breast and plopped it over the top of her bra.

Jimmy gasped. "What're you doing? You can't do that, you're my doctor!"

Miss Smith smiled. 'It's all part of your therapy, Jimmy. It's called Mothering Nurturing. I am 100% certain your mother did not breast feed you and this failure is a principal factor in your general dis-ease and inability to choose a suitable mate. Put the tip of your tongue on my nipple."

"No, Miss Smith, this is impossible. It's just not right!" He felt a budding paranoia creeping through the nitrous oxide and marijuana high. "This isn't some kind of trick is it?" He jumped to his feet, swaying slightly with the sudden motion. "You're going to have me arrested!"

"Jimmy, sit back down," the doctor said in a soft but forceful voice. "Why would I want to do something like that? What possible benefit would that have for either one of us? You are my patient and I am your doctor and my only concern is your welfare and well-being. Now sit down, breathe slowly in and out, relax, and look at my nipple."

Jimmy sat down and looked, feeling his paranoia easing and his libido increasing.

"That's a very big nipple," he commented. "It looks kind of hard."

Miss Smith smiled. "And it can get even harder. Now put your tongue on it. That's good, Jimmy, very good. Now lick it gently. Gently, gently. That's it. Suck on it softly. Softly, Jimmy, softly. That's very nice, very nice. I knew you could do it." A low moan rose from her throat. "That's a good boy, such a good boy. Oh, yes, yes, now here, suck on the other one." She undid her bra, freeing both breasts. Jimmy moved his mouth to her right breast, squeezing the left while passing his thumb back and forth over the nipple. "Oh, God," she groaned, "that just feels so good, so good, Jimmy! Keep going, keep going, keep go-" The doctor began bucking violently from the hips, twisting her head and shoulders and arching her back as her upper chest and throat turned from light pink to almost crimson. "OK, Jimmy, OK, alright, alright, gaad gaad gaad, that's enough now, Johnny Johnny stop now," she spluttered. "Please you have to stop now!" she cried, grabbing him by the hair, pulling his head back and pushing him away so hard he had to grab hold of the desk to keep from falling. She quickly buttoned her blouse, stood up and briskly shook Jimmy's limp hand. "I'm very sorry but the session is over," she said, "you're making excellent progress. Please make an appointment for two weeks at the reception desk. Thank you for coming. I'm looking forward to seeing you again. I'll have a nice surprise for you when you come back."

Jimmy walked shakily to the door and paused before opening it. Wait a minute, he thought. Did she just call me Johnny?

For the third time that day Miss Smith smoked a pinch of pot. Then she raised the second balloon to her lips and drained it.

Chapter Forty-Two

REPORTING BACK

Once again Dr. Mendelssohn found himself addressing guests sitting in his living room. "Now, we know that nobody had any success with the hand staring technique we tried last time we were here, but it's been a couple weeks since then and I'm sure some of you were unable to refrain from smoking in that length of time," he said to general laughter. "So. Did anybody manage to come back from a trip with at least a modicum of memory of what happened when they were there?"

Bob turned to Bill. "Modicum?"

"A little bit," Bill whispered back.

Mendelssohn frowned. "No one? That is disheartening."

"How's Anna doing?"asked Charles.

"I'm afraid that's a little disheartening, too. No change. But at least she's still eating and sleeping OK and there's been no change for the worse. So I guess that's good,"he sighed.

For once no one felt much like getting high, so after a few beers and snacks, everyone headed out. "John, could you hang out a little longer?" Mendelssohn asked his friend as he was leaving. "You said you'd been having some interesting experiences and I think it's time we talked about that. I'll be right back."

John sat down on the couch. A minute later the doctor returned, leading Anna by the hand and they sat on the love seat facing him. John shot them a startled look.

Mendelssohn returned John's gaze, turned to Anna, then looked back at John. "I honestly don't know if I'm doing the right thing here." He rubbed the back of his neck and sighed. "But you know how the Pletz boys were apparently largely responsible for drawing Anna out of her coma, maybe because they were carrying on and making noise, who knows. What I do know is that I haven't had any success getting through to her since she came to stay here in spite of all the talking I've done with her. I've talked to her about everything from baseball to politics, about our favorite movies and TV shows, about music, I play her favorite Charlie Parker recordings, nothing, she has no reaction to anything. But there is one fact that I think carries some weight. She started acting strangely right after she tried DMT for the first time. So maybe if you talk about your experiences it might ring some kind of bell with her. I figured it's worth a try. And anyhow I'm curious to hear what kind of stuff happened to you." He laughed. "Now I'll shut up and hear what you have to say."

"Hell, Doc," John began, "if you think it'll help, sure." He looked at Anna, who was staring blankly into space. "Anyhow, I've been wanting to tell somebody about it because it just seems so fucking weird, I kind of wonder if anyone else has these experiences like I do. I'm not even sure why, but I only felt like telling Syndy a little about it but this seems like the perfect time to get it all off my chest, especially if you think it might do your girl some good. So, I guess I'll start from the beginning.

"I really enjoyed myself at first with all the jewels and flashing lights and stuff,the things everybody sees. But then it seemed like Gunge was getting a little too deep inside my head."

"Gunge?" Mendelssohn interrupted.

"Yeah, that's the name of the guy who seems to be the leader. I don't know how I found out his name, it just seemed to come into my mind. That's the spooky part, he seems to have some kind of control over my mind, like I would feel the sudden urge to smoke and then when I did he would insinuate that he had made me do it. Then when I started bitching about how lousy my life was he said he could make it better, give me everything I wanted. And it was either a coincidence or else he really does have powers to affect our world because I hooked up with Syndy not long after I complained about not having a woman." John stopped talking and looked at the floor.

"Go on," Mendelssohn urged. "What's wrong? It's just getting interesting."

"Uh, Doc, I feel really bad about this. I know I should have told you a long time ago but I just couldn't bring myself to do it. I'm so fucking ashamed of myself."

"C'mon, John, it's OK, whatever it is I'm sure it's not as bad as you think. Out with it, spill it, I promise I won't get mad."

"I sold you out!"John sobbed. "He told me all my dreams would come true if I got my friends to smoke. And then he wanted Anna and then he wanted Tony!"

"No no no!" Anna screamed. "No no no!"

Chapter Forty-Three

SARAH AND JIMMY

Two days after Jimmy made his appointment Miss Sarah Smith called him to change where he would be seeing her. On the appointed day he entered the designated building on the Upper West Side, took the elevator to the sixth floor and was let into apartment 606 by its kimono clad occupant. "Welcome, Jimmy," Miss Smith whispered, "make yourself at home." Jimmy walked into the middle of the living room, stopped and turned.

"This is your apartment, not a doctor's office," he stated.

"That's right, Jimmy. I think you'll be much more comfortable here," Miss Smith replied. Taking a seat at the bar and lighting a cigarette she propped her left foot on the stool to her side. Her kimono slid open enough to reveal that she wasn't wearing panties. "May I ask you a question?" she said. "What do you think of me?"

Jimmy whistled a long, slowly descending note. "Oh, my God!" he crowed. "You are really something else, Miss Smith, or should I say, 'Mrs. Robinson?'"

Miss Smith took three quick steps toward him, laughed, veered sharply to the right and glided behind the bar. "I'm sure I have no idea what you mean, Jimmy," she replied. "Say, what would you like to drink? I'm having a martini. Doesn't that sound good?"

Jimmy took out a joint, lit it, took a long toke, walked over to the bar and extended his arm.

"Yeah, I think it'll go very nicely with this," he said, exhaling smoke in her face.

She caressed his hand as she accepted his offer. "Umm, that does have an excellent aroma," she said, putting it in her mouth. "I see you know how to whistle, don't you Jimmy? I know how to whistle too, Jimmy," she added, the joint bobbing between her lips. She came around the bar, took his hand and led him slowly toward the back of the apartment. "You just put your lips together and...blow. It can be a highly useful skill."

As they lay in bed later, post coital cigarettes in hand, Jimmy commented, "I guess this means I can't be your patient anymore, what with the general frowning of society on doctor/patient sexual relationships."

"Oh, you'll still be my patient," Miss Smith replied, "I have lots more therapy to share with you,i t'll just be a little more personal and off the books. And I still have to show you that surprise I promised you."

"I thought the surprise was your pussy."

"You liked that didn't you? You were very enthusiastic. But I think you'll find this very enjoyable as well. I've been saving it for dessert." She ambled with an exaggerated bump and grind to her dresser, took out two pipes and hopped back into bed. "Let me introduce you," she murmured, "to a whole world of surprises."

Chapter Forty-Four

Anna Speaks

"That goddamn motherfucking son of a bitch!" Anna shrieked. She dove onto the couch, legs kicking and arms flailing. "That cocksucking scumbag! That fucking shithead! I'll kill him! I'll fucking kill him with my bare hands!" Mendelssohn tried to encircle her with his arms while John held her legs but both gave up when her hits and kicks started hitting home.

"Just let her get it out," the doctor advised, backing away. "John, do me a favor, bring a wet washcloth from the bathroom and a glass of water while I keep an eye on her."

By the time John got back Anna's screams had turned into sobs she was burying in the pillows. Mendelssohn managed to get her into an upright position and daubed her forehead with the washcloth. She took a couple sips of water and lay back down. "I'm sorry," she said softly, covering her eyes with her arm. "I always seem to be saying I'm sorry."

"Hey, baby, don't worry, I'm a big boy now and I've been around the block a few times,"Mendelssohn joked, adjusting her pillow. "Hell, I've heard that kind of language at least a couple times before, on TV. It's amazing what they get away with these days on network television."

Anna laughed and took the washcloth to wipe her eyes. "Oh, Gene, Gene, you're so good to me," she said, pulling him down to her with a hug. "I don't deserve you, I really don't."

"No, of course you don't, honey," the doctor smiled, "but if we keep working on you maybe some day you will." He gave her a long kiss on the forehead. "Now, why don't you go lie down on the bed for a while and get some rest? I'm going to talk with John for a bit and then I'll come in and join you. Wait, I think you need a little boost there," he added, pulling her gently by the arms as she struggled to get up. "Let's go now, nice and slow, easy does it, let's go right back to bed for a little nap."

Mendelssohn returned to the couch shaking his head. "I'm really at a loss to figure out what's going on with her," he confessed to John. "This is the second time she's gone off the deep end and it's got me baffled."

"But Doc, you should be happy!" John pointed out. "Not only did she come out of her coma but now she's talking again! Well, maybe not exactly talking, more cursing like a sailor, but still..."

Mendelssohn gave him a hard look but then laughed. "You're right, the good thing is that she's back with us again. Not in the best of shape, but she's back. She could have stayed in that coma and died, for Christ's sake!"

"You know what amazes me, Doc? She was practically hysterical and then she calmed down so suddenly."

"Thank God for that! I think it's because she's still so weak and that outburst exhausted her."

John nodded toward the bedroom. "You didn't get a chance to talk with her back there, did you, to get a clue what it's all about?"

"No, man, I didn't want to risk triggering another episode at this point, there's plenty of time for that. I'm anxious to see what she'll be like when she wakes up, if she'll be able to talk calmly about what's bothering her or if she's gonna clam up again. That possibility really has me worried."

"Uh, you know I feel shitty, 'cause you know, just maybe it was kinda my fault."

"Your fault? How could it be your fault?"

"Well, remember I was telling you I sold you out because Gunge said he'd give me everything if I got Anna and Tony to smoke?"

"Yeah..."

"Well, that's exactly when Anna started freaking out, when she heard me say that, don't you remember?"

"Right, right, that's when she started screaming, of course! But why would that upset her so much? She was perfectly willing to try DMT even though she didn't get much out of it. Hell, John, I don't feel like you sold anybody out and I don't see why she would either. It doesn't make any sense."

"But she was mad as hell, Doc. She said, 'That son of a bitch, I'll kill him with my bare hands,' didn't she?"

"Yeah, yeah, but why would she want to kill Gunge? If I don't know who he is, how would she since she barely remembers anything after she smokes? And how could she possibly kill him even if she wanted to?"

"I don't know, man, you're just going to have to talk to her. You might wanna have some kind of tranquilizers on hand when you do, though, in case she blows up again. Wait a minute, on second thought pills might not be too good an idea. Hell, Doc, I'm sorry, I just don't know what to say except good luck!"

CHAPTER FORTY-FIVE

LUNCH AT BABBALUCCI

Jimmy took a bite of his pizza and wiped his mouth with exaggerated politeness. "Say now, my dear, do tell the truth," he said in a Stewie from Family Guy voice, "do you find this eggplant topping to your liking?"

"Why, it's simply mahvelous," Miss Smith replied, sipping from her beer glass with one pinky extended. "I'm absolutely so delighted you had the perspicacity to think of it. But must one use one's hands on these slippery slices? I do so feel that proper sanitation should call for knife and fork."

"Go ahead!" Jimmy laughed. "You're not Mayor de Blasio, so you don't have to worry about fighting off a shit storm of public opinion."

"Oh, yeah, I remember that! I believe opinions came out on both sides of the question but let's face it, Jimmy, who gives a damn about what other people think? Of all the people who come in to lie down on my leather couch, 99 percent are there because they let other people screw with their minds. From the minute we're born we're pressured by everyone from parents to teachers to classmates to do well and conform to what they think we should be. You know where all that crap comes from? From hundreds of thousands of years ago, when, if you were a loner and didn't pull your weight in your tribe, you were ostracized and wound up dead. It's hardwired. Look at any high school. Everybody wants to be popular so they do what they think their friends think is cool instead of just being themselves by acting and dressing the way that feels natural to them. But it's no longer necessary. In fact, in the broader view we find the most respected people throughout history are the ones who weren't afraid to be different and pioneered a new way. That's one of the things I like about drugs. They open your mind to different ways of looking at things and peel back the bullshit to get at the real truth inside each one of us."

"Don't look now, Sarah, but your pizza's getting cold."

"Oh, so you don't agree with me."

"No, I think you make some good points but your pizza's getting cold." Jimmy finished his slice. "Just sayin'."

"OK, OK, end of lecture. Anyhow, I know you think the same way I do about drugs. Everyone who uses them does it for the pleasure, obviously, but a lot more people are starting to realize their therapeutic effects. I don't think it'll be too long before psilocybin and LSD will be the go-to drugs in therapy sessions."

"Not DMT?"

"What do you think?"

"Ha! No fucking way! I don't trust this Gunge character. What's his story, anyway? I can't make heads or tails of him."

"Me either. The only thing that seems to be for sure is that he totally rules his little kingdom."

"But what the hell is that kingdom? All the gems and flashing lights and words becoming solid objects. What does it all mean? And where is it? Is it an alternate universe or is it in our heads or what?"

Miss Smith reached across the table, covering Jimmy's hand with her own.

"That's what's so exciting! Nobody knows! Maybe we can be the pioneers, the first to come to grips with this phenomenon for the benefit of all mankind!"

Jimmy shot his arms out like a preacher. "To serve man!"

"That's it, Jimmy, that's what I'm talking about!"

"No, babe," he laughed. "Don't you get it? Don't you remember the Twilight Zone where the aliens come to earth and say they want to serve man but what they really mean is they wanna serve us up as food?"

"Oh, yeah, that was a great episode!"

"Well, think about it. I don't know if Gunge and his cohorts are aliens or what, but I have some serious doubts that they have our best interests at heart. Just from that one time I got a really weird vibe from those jokers. All the posing and shapeshifting and dazzling stuff, you know, look at me, look what I can do."

"Should we have another go at it and see if we can figure it out?"

"Uh, I'm not quite up for another visit to crazy town just yet. I have a better idea. Why don't we adjourn to my place and we can mellow out with a little weed?"

***

Jimmy and Miss Smith lay on their backs on his bed passing a corncob pipe filled with pot between them. "You know something, Sarah," Jimmy remarked, handing her the pipe. "You're the best thing that ever happened to me. You're not only beautiful and smart but you're also my free fountain of 24/7 psychotherapy."

Miss Smith raised herself on one elbow, put her face a foot away from Jimmy's and faked a frown. "I think that's all you care about, mister. You're definitely taking advantage of my good nature."

"You have a big nose," Jimmy remarked.

"Yeah, that's right," Miss Smith replied and pushed her nose into Jimmy's, using hers to slap his back and forth. "You know what they say about women who have big noses, don't you?"

He managed to shake his head no despite the onslaught.

"They have big clits!" she shouted, pinning him by the shoulders to the bed.

"That's the way uh huh uh huh I like it," Jimmy sang and struggled to get up. He managed to free his right arm enough to reach for her crotch.

"Oh, no you don't!" laughed Miss Smith, slapping his hand away. "No more sex for you! Not after that comment about my nose. That comment reveals that you are a very troubled man and I think we should have a little therapy session right here and now. You lie back down on the bed and I'm going to lie down right next to you, but no touching. You got it? No touching!"

"OK," Jimmy grumbled and they lay down again by her side.

"Now then, what's troubling you, young man?" Miss Smith began.

"Who says there's anything troubling me? Why should anything be troubling me?"

"C'mon, Jimmy, everybody has problems. I know I'm quite an excellent therapist and therefore you're doing much better now, but you're not completely cured. Out with it."

"Well, you know I like women."

"That's good to know Jimmy, but even if you were gay we could still be friends."

"Very funny. But what I mean is, and I don't want you to get jealous 'cause you have no reason to, I'm very happy with you, I'm crazy about you and I don't want anyone else but you but I do find other women attractive and I like to look at them."

"I'm shocked, shocked at such a thing! That is so abnormal that I'm going to pretend you never said it. That's the only way I'll be able to survive. In all my years of practice I've never heard of such a thing. Nowhere never ever heard of it. It is simply so-"

"Alright, alright, Jesus Christ, Sarah, can you let me get a word in edgewise for Christ's sake?"

"That's twice in one short sentence you took the Lord's name in vain. Twice."

"Since when did you become so religious?"

"Jesus, Jimmy, for Christ's sake lighten up! You said we were going to mellow out, but you're all uptight."

"I'm sorry, it's just that sometimes I can't tell if you're serious. We haven't been together that long and let's face it, we're still getting to know each other."

"You're right, and I'm sorry too. So let's in fact get to know each other a little better. Tell me, what is it about women that's bothering you?"

"I don't understand them."

"Join the club. Not even women understand women."

"Alright, but you must have some insight into them, especially as a psychologist. So here's what I don't get. Like I said, I like to look at women and everybody likes to be noticed, so it's a nice feeling when on rare occasion someone looks back. But whether anyone looks back or not doesn't seem to be based on any factors I can come up with. Sometimes an eternity can go by where I'm completely invisible and then for a brief time I'm a movie star, attracting glances left and right and then suddenly I'm back on the cutting room floor. It doesn't matter how I'm feeling or what I'm wearing or the time of day or anything I can put my finger on."

Miss Smith refilled the pipe and took a hit. "It could be pheromones."

"You know, I thought that too. I read a book about the vomeronasal organ that supposedly deals with pheromones but I'm talking about outdoors, so I don't think that explains it. And it often happens when the woman is pretty far away."

"Hmm."

"And sometimes they'll turn around like they sense someone's looking at them. Even when I'm not looking at them. African women are the best at that."

"How do you know they're African and not African-American or Jamaican or Haitian?"

"The posture, the graceful way of walking. Sometimes long, colorful clothes, which are a dead give-away, of course."

"I see. Well, let me think about this for a second." Miss Smith raised both arms, put her palms together, then opened them, then lowered them to cover the top of her head. She breathed slowly in and out for a full minute. Jimmy reached for the pipe and lit it. "Ah ha!" Miss Smith suddenly cried out, shooting out her arms and knocking the pipe from Jimmy's hands.

"I've got it! You have magneton-antimagneton diverse membrane attraction syndrome, Jimmy! Definitely! Of course, it can only be understood fully in a contextual study of astrophysics, astronomy, astrology, quantum theory and the relative stages of the menstrual cycles of the women in your immediate sector, but I think we've got a pretty good handle on it now.Those embers didn't burn the bedspread too badly did they? Good! Because," she added, unbuttoning Jimmy's shirt, "you are unquestionably in the magneton stage at this very minute and there's not a nanosecond of time to be wasted!"

Chapter Forty-Six

THE TRUTH COMES OUT

When Anna woke up on her left side, she slowly opened her eyes to see that Dr. Mendelssohn, on his right side, was staring intently into her face. She sat up and pulled herself closer. "Gene, what's wrong? Has something happened?"

"You were talking in your sleep."

"I was? What did I say?"

Mendelssohn continued to stare. Anna began to shake. Wrapping his arms around her he pushed her back down onto the bed with his full weight on top and put his mouth next to her ear. "Easy,

Anna, easy, easy, I've got you now, no one can hurt you."

"Kill him for me, Gene! Kill him! Kill him!"

"Shh, shh, don't you worry, baby," Mendelssohn whispered, "he'll get what's coming to him."

***

When John met his friend at the Harlem Shake Shack on Lenox Avenue and 124th Street it was immediately apparent that Dr. Mendelssohn was even more upset than he'd sounded on the phone. "Jesus, Doc, you look terrible, what's going on?" he asked, leaning forward to put his arms on the table. "You said it was serious, but, man, you look like your dog just died. Oh, shit, that's not it, it's Anna, isn't it? What happened? Is she OK?"

"He raped her, John!"Mendelssohn screamed, slamming his hand down repeatedly on the table. "He raped her! He raped her!"

John threw his arm around him and pulled him to his feet. "C'mon, Doc," he said, "let's go for a walk."

Walking quickly down Lenox Avenue, dodging the other pedestrians, John kept his arm around the doctor and attempted with some success to pacify his outbursts until they reached Central Park.

They wound up sitting on a bench facing the lake, looking out at the geese and turtles. After the long walk Mendelssohn had calmed down. "The problem is, John, we have no proof of anything. All Anna can remember is that she woke up in a strange bed and Tony Bunson walked in naked from the bathroom. She doesn't remember where the room was, she has no idea how they met up, she can't even say for certain that they had sex, but I know he raped her, John, I just know he did!"

"And of course there's no sperm sample or anything like that," John added, "because the next thing we know she's in a coma, right Doc?"

Mendelssohn clenched his fists. "My God, if she hadn't come out of that coma that bastard would have got away with not only rape but murder too!"

"He's not gonna get away with it, Doc, I promise he's not gonna get away with it!"

"John, John, John," the doctor sighed, his own anger waning as John's rose. "I've talked to so many lawyers and they all say the same thing. We don't have a case. I don't know why I get so worked up about this when I know it's hopeless, but it just burns me up inside knowing there's nothing we can do."

"Jesus, Doc, the reason you get so worked up is because you love her and because that fuckhead Tony is a peace of shit! Don't give in! Stay angry! Fuck the lawyers and the courts! We don't need them. This is all my fault and I'm gonna see that justice is done!"

CHAPTER FORTY-SEVEN

THE WEDDING

James Harold Hanson married Sarah Elizabeth Smith on a partly cloudy Wednesday at 3 o'clock in the afternoon in a small church in uptown Manhattan. They both wore white; John a three piece linen suit and Sarah, who chose to leave the name "Miss Smith" in the past, her mother's wedding dress. The next day the Hansons boarded a flight to Maui, checked in at the Hyatt Regency and proceeded to comb Lahaina for souvenirs and herb. They were successful on both fronts and were particularly pleased with the wide variety of pot they came up with. But after two weeks of being almost continually stoned they were ready to return to New York. "Babe," Jimmy remarked, "I think if we keep this up I will be sporting two fried organs. Brain and skin."

When they got back home Sarah jumped back into her practice and Jimmy, not sure how to spend his time as a married man with no job, coasted back into his old habit of poking about the streets of Harlem. "Just till I figure out what to do with myself," he promised his wife. "I'm not really looking at women anymore, I'm just studying the scene," he added.

"Jimmy, I don't expect you not to look at women, I'd be pretty worried if you didn't," Sarah replied. "You can look at the menu as long as you don't place an order. So go ahead and play the flaneur. But why don't you consider taking up a hobby of some sort?"

"What, stamp collecting, tropical fish? I did all that stuff when I was a kid, that's a drag. Although now that I think of it a nice 50 gallon salt water tank might look kinda nice when we move into the condo."

"Sure, why not. But you're doing all the dirty work."

"Or, you know what? I'm kinda interested in psychiatry. Maybe I could sit in on some of your sessions."

"Tell you what, Jimmy, why don't I just lend you a couple of books instead?"

Chapter Forty-Eight

THE ASSAULT

Nobody was to get hurt. John emphasized that fact when he met with the Pletz brothers in his apartment to discuss his plan. "So what's the point then?" Bill wanted to know. "We don't have to kill him but we should at least rough the motherfucker up good, don't you think? I mean he did rape Anna, even if there's no proof. That's what the doc says, right?"

"Yeah, that's right, but, uh, speaking of the doc it's better not to say anything to him about this, OK? So here's what we do. We're gonna paint "RAPIST" in big red letters on the front door of the tavern. And if you guys think you can get inside we can stir things around a bit in there too. You know, no serious damage but just rearrange the furniture and the bottles, maybe some nice graffiti in the restrooms, things like that.Whatever we come up with on the spot. Are you in?"

"Yeah, damn straight we're in!" they both answered at once.

They met up at Tony's at 5 am. While John painted the front door Bob managed to break in through the back door and began emptying liquor bottles, refilling them with water. Using John's paint Bill blotted out the appropriate letters from the Tony's Tavern sign to make it say "Tons ave." "That'll learn the fat ass motherfucker," he laughed.

But while the three of them were doing that, Tony Bunson and his security guards Emilio and Joseph Gonzalez were being awakened in their respective homes by the silent alarm Tony had installed shortly after the poker game fiasco.

Living just a few blocks away, he was the first to arrive at the Tavern and when he saw what was on his front door he drove his fist into it with such force that his hand shattered.

Unfazed, he flung the door open and burst into the bar with a roar that caused John to let go of the bottle of cognac he was swigging from and fall to the floor. Running up to him like a kid at bat in a kickball game, Tony cocked his knee a foot from John's head but was felled by John as he spun on his back and sliced Tony's leg open with the jagged edge of the broken bottle. The Pletz brothers sprang out of the restrooms in the back and were pummeling Tony in the face and ribs when the Gonzalez brothers showed up with guns drawn and began shooting at the ceiling. Scrambling to escape, Bob Pletz knocked into Emilio Gonzalez, who was still firing away. A bullet entered Tony Bunson's heart. When the police arrived minutes later, they found John, Emilio, Joseph, and a lifeless Tony.

Chapter Forty-Nine

THE ARREST

John was taken to the 26th Precinct along with the Gonzalez brothers, who insisted there were two other men despite John's insistence that he was the only one involved. The brothers were released pending further investigation, which revealed there had in fact been accomplices, which John then admitted, but he still refused to name them. The Gonzalez brothers, who had gun permits, were reprimanded for negligent use of a firearm but the shooting of Bunson was deemed unintentional and charges against them were dropped.

As the case against John Camry progressed and became more widely known, the Pletz brothers, unable to deal with the guilt of letting their friend bear the entire blame, turned themselves in. At trial everything came out. Both Dr. Mendelssohn and Anna were questioned and absolved of all responsibility. John remained silent on everyone's use of drugs except his own and Tony's and his lawyer based his defense on John's certainty that he was to blame for the rape because he had introduced Tony to DMT and it was his duty to do something about it. Based on statements during his interrogation and his written testimony that Gunge was affecting his behavior and had extraordinary powers of control over him, he was sent for psychiatric evaluation, diagnosed as bipolar, and remanded to Bellevue for further observation. Under the sponsorship of Dr. Mendelssohn Bob and Bill Pletz escaped jail time and were given 6 months community service.

CHAPTER FIFTY

FIVE YEARS LATER

J ennifer Elizabeth Hanson shook her curly hair and admired her bright yellow with red polka dots dress in the full view mirror. Pulling it wide from both sides she turned to the left, turned to the right and then spun around as fast as she could, trying to catch from the corner of her eye the effect her slip made as it rose with the dress to create a sunset bordered by white clouds. The doorbell rang. "It must be Auntie!" she yelled down the hallway. "I'll get it!"

When she flung open the door her Aunt Jan scooped her up in her arms and lifted her high over her head. "Oh, my," she laughed, "you're getting to be so big now, Jenny, I can hardly pick you up anymore!"

"Piggyback, Auntie, piggyback!" the child pleaded and her aunt obligingly placed her on her shoulders, plodded slowly once around the living room and stopped to catch her breath.

"Again, Auntie, again!" Jennifer shouted, pulling on her aunt's hair.

"Ouch, Jenny, that hurts," she complained, placing her on the floor. "I'm afraid your old auntie just doesn't have it in her for another race around the track. But wait a minute, what's this on the table? It's so beautiful!"

"Auntie you know what that is, it's my birthday cake and it has four candles!"

"Why, yes, it does, I told you you were getting to be a big girl now. But you're not big enough to be home all alone, where's mommy and daddy?"

Jennifer began walking around the table, admiring the cake from different angles. "They're getting dressed," she replied, continuing to circle the cake while softly humming a tune.

"What's that you're humming, sweetie?"

"Oh, it's a very nice song. You want me to sing it for you?"

"Oh, of course, honey."

"OK, it goes like this. You are my sunshine, my only sunshine, you make me happy when skies are gray, you'll never know, dear, how much I love you, please don't take my sunshine away."

"Oh, yes, that is a nice song. Did your mommy teach you that?"

"Oh, no, Mommy never sings anymore," she frowned, then smiled shyly. "I'll tell you how I learned it." The tiny smile grew, at first imperceptibly, then swiftly taking over her face, leaving her mouth wide open and teeth gleaming. Her eyes flashed. Jumping straight up she spun 360 degrees, landed, jumped up again while furiously clapping her hands and came down with a loud smack. She threw back her head.

"Gunge taught it to me!" she howled. "It was Gunge!"

MY THANKS TO BECA, MARIE AND
ARTHUR FOR THEIR TIME, PATIENCE
AND TECHNICAL EXPERTISE

www.ingramcontent.com/pod-product-compliance
Lightning Source LLC
Chambersburg PA
CBHW071125170626
46809CB00002B/496